I0671123

CROCODILE ISLAND

CROCODILE ISLAND

From The Secret Diary of Eddie Ocean

E.O. TEST

**A WHIMSICAL FANTASY ADVENTURE FOR YOUNG
ADULTS
AND OTHER
WISTFUL PEOPLE**

Copyright © 2015 Edgar O. Test
All rights reserved.

ISBN: 0985305010
ISBN 13: 9780985305017

AUTHORS NOTE

Disclaimer: This is a work of fiction. Any incidents herein involving real people are fictitious and should not be assumed to be true depictions of their character or behavior or of incidents that actually occurred.

ACKNOWLEDGMENTS

I want to acknowledge my late mother who, when I was a youngster, unleashed my imagination through her well-imagined and well-told stories about being an Indian princess, and tales about her living in the days of the *Arabian Nights*.

I want to acknowledge my late father for instilling a sense of humor in me by often coming home from work and telling me the jokes that he had heard that day.

I'm grateful for my always-supportive wife Margaret, son Matt, and daughter Raegan. I can't forget my five sisters, Judy, Toni, Julie, Karen, and Rhonda; from them I gained valuable insight into the female psyche while growing up in Kentucky.

Finally, I'm most grateful for the professional services provided by my editor Cynthia MacGregor who offered both encouragement and thoughtful suggestions.

TABLE OF CONTENTS

BOOK #1

CROCODILE ISLAND

BY

E. O. TEST

Crocodile Island is a whimsical, fantasy adventure that takes place in South Florida during the 1970s.

Autobiographical threads are woven throughout the tapestry of my tall tale. The humor is probably appropriate for young adults but not children.

Chapter 1

MAROONED ON CROCODILE ISLAND

Born near Detroit, Michigan, I grew up in Kentucky and went to college in Philadelphia, Pennsylvania. I have always had a restless soul, an urge to move on from place to place and job to job. I did not find peace until I moved near the Atlantic Ocean. Maybe that has something to do with my name. I'm Eddie Ocean, and this is my secret diary.

SATURDAY, APRIL 1ST, 1972

It was 1972 when I first arrived in Miami, Florida. I was a landlubber and enough of a fool to decide to buy a boat and become a sea captain. For some reason I had always been drawn to the sea but knew little about her. Fortunately, I met an old Cuban sea captain, who for forty years had transported watermelons from Homestead, Florida to Nassau in the Bahamas. He had decided to retire and offered his boat for sale. Her name was the *Watermelon*.

The *Watermelon* was an old 26-foot wooden boat built in Nova Scotia, Canada by a master craftsman and shipwright. She had a very wide beam of 12 feet, which made the craft appear to be oval shaped.

With a small cuddy cabin forward, she was comfortable and very seaworthy, plus she could haul heavy loads safely. The boat had a single diesel motor and one mast that could carry a bit of sail.

The crazy old captain had painted the hull green, the deck and cabin red. Then he painted black dots all over the red deck and cabin making the little boat look like a watermelon that had been cut in half and set afloat on the ocean. He considered his boat the perfect craft for transporting tons of watermelons from Florida to Nassau.

MONDAY, MAY 1ST, 1972

I was able to buy the *Watermelon* for a very low price. The old man loved his boat and demanded that anyone who bought her must swear an oath to keep her painted like a watermelon and not change her name. The tough, local longshoremen and seamen of Miami did not want to be caught dead piloting that funny-looking boat around the pirate-infested Atlantic Ocean and Caribbean Sea!

Not having much money and being new to this business, I swallowed my pride and agreed to take care of the old man's beloved vessel. I paid the weather-beaten old sea captain every penny I had, and he happily accepted the pittance, which amounted to only a fraction of the boat's true value. He was happy with the sale because he knew that I would care for his beloved vessel. As part of the deal, the old man agreed to teach me seamanship and show me his trading route for one month. We shook hands, and I became the new owner of the *Watermelon*.

TUESDAY JUNE 6TH, 1972

After one month of training, I became captain and made my first solo crossing to the Bahamas. I assumed the old man's shipping business, hauling supplies and watermelons from the Florida mainland and the Keys to our neighbors in the Bahamas. I would return to America with Bahamian exports.

I captained the *Watermelon* for over a year, barely eking out a living wage by hauling goods and passengers around the Florida Keys and the Bahamas. My home base was Miami, and I could have made much more money by working as a radiographer at Jackson Memorial Hospital, but the freedom and adventure that came with being an independent boat captain pleased me. I had become addicted to a life aquatic. Saltwater flowed through my veins now, and there would be no going back to the landlubber's lifestyle. Every day was like waking up on vacation and looking forward to the next adventure, not rising to go to a dreaded job. In July of 1973, a series of unfortunate events temporarily interrupted my idyllic lifestyle and altered the course of my destiny forevermore.

THURSDAY JULY 20TH, 1973

One lovely but hot summer day, on my return voyage from Nassau and only a few miles from my port of destination, my journey was unexpectedly interrupted. After rounding Marathon Key and entering the Gulf of Mexico, the *Watermelon* experienced a sudden bump and a jolt, causing her to shudder and slow to a stop.

"How could I have run aground out here?" I wondered as I peered over the side into the emerald green water. I knew that the Gulf was at least 50 feet deep at this location.

Confused, I walked to the stern and looked down at the propeller, only to be startled to see a big, green head shaped like a parrot's beak protruding from the water. With black, bead eyes, the creature stared up at me from the ocean.

"What the heck!" I said as I jumped backward, scared near to death.

I calmed down when I realized that the head belonged to a harmless giant green sea turtle. The huge turtle was also unsettled from our open water encounter.

His expression seemed to be asking me, *What did you do that for?*

"Sorry, turtle! I guess this ocean isn't big enough for both of us!" I yelled sarcastically.

It's true that when one spends too much time alone at sea, one is prone to talk to himself, his boat, or any creature that might listen.

I was happy to see the turtle dive below the surface and swim away unharmed, flipping me off with his tail as he dove.

"I guess you're not one for conversation, eh? I said.

I returned to the helm of my little boat. She was loaded at the bow with straw hats and piles of coconut seeds that the Bahamians had carved to resemble hairy, screaming monkey heads. Tourists from the North, especially New Jersey and New York, bought these Bahamian monkey head sculptures by the dozens. Below deck, the cuddy cabin was filled to the brim with cases of Kalik Ale destined for Sloppy Joe's Pub and the Monster nightclub in Key West.

I put my boat into drive and throttled forward, but she did not move. I checked the stern again and this time noticed that my propeller was broken!

"Thanks a lot, turtle!" I yelled at the ocean. "Your shell must be as hard as a rock! Thanks a lot!"

I had a spare prop but knew I could not safely make the repair out here in the Gulf of Mexico, so I sat down to look at my navigation charts. Hoisting my sail in this dead calm would be a waste of time. Luckily a strong westerly current was pushing my craft on a course that I calculated would pass near a small-uninhabited Island called *Isla de los Cocodrilos del Toro.* This is the Spanish name that the explorer Ponce de Leon had given that place when his expedition first discovered it in the year 1493. The English translation is roughly *Island of Bull Crocodiles.*

Huge, vicious bull crocodiles once inhabited this island, and several members of de Leon's party were taken during the night and devoured when the giant reptiles attacked them as they slept. Even armed with muskets and daggers, the Spaniards were forced to retreat and flee the island, vowing never to return. On their charts, they marked the island with the skull and crossbones symbol, a danger warning to all seafarers.

Comforted by the knowledge that years ago trappers had killed all the crocodiles, I planned to beach my boat on Crocodile Island so that I could fix my propeller. My drift and wind calculations put my ETA at about three hours hence. Since I was now at the mercy of the ocean current, I put on one of the oversized Bahamian straw hats and sat down in a shady spot to hydrate myself. I had the good habit of hydrating to excess, the best way to combat the effect of the Florida heat and blazing sun.

I drank for over an hour, filling the transom with empty Kalik cans before I fell asleep. Two hours into my nap I awoke to the sound of gentle surf and could see a lush tropical island off my port beam. I grabbed one of my dock lines and jumped into the waist-deep water, pulling the *Watermelon* toward the beach. The sun was setting now, and I knew that I would not be able to finish my prop repair before dark.

With the cuddy cabin full of cases of Kalik Ale, the bow of the boat loaded with straw hats and carved monkey heads, and the stern littered with empty ale cans, I found no desirable place to sleep, so I grabbed my pup tent and went ashore to make camp.

The island had an eerie calm; the place was creepy! I decided to string empty Kalik cans onto some fishing line and hang them just above the ground around the perimeter of my campsite, forming a crude alarm system. If someone approached me during the night, they would trip on the string of cans, which would sound a warning alarm.

Late that night, inside my tent, I awoke from a deep sleep to clinking sounds. The noise became frantic; someone or something was tangled in my trip line. I dove head first from my tent and immediately saw a huge croc. Distracted, the big bull was thrashing its tail and snapping at the string of cans tangled around its body until it saw me. The laserlike focus of his fire-red eyes burned a hole into my soul.

"Oh my God! Help me!" I spoke out loud as the reptile, crouching low, began to cautiously approach me with a choppy marching gait.

I scrambled to my feet, realizing that the clever beast had cut off my route of escape. He was standing between the *Watermelon* and me; I couldn't make a run for it! As a teenager, I had spent a summer in Hollywood, Florida with Seminole Indians wrestling alligators to entertain tourists. I began to use the wrestling moves that I had learned from the Seminoles. I knew these grappling techniques were very effective on a common alligator. I did not know if the moves would be as effective on this huge, mutant beast, this "crocodile of bull alligator."

I feinted to the left, tossed a sand clod directly over the beast's head, and then moved quickly to my right, prepared to leap onto the monster's back while his head was still turned away. He was too fast, lightning fast, and he almost decapitated me! His jaws snapped shut with a loud clap as I spun in midair to evade the deadly teeth.

Hurtling through the air, I pulled my head down and away just in time. The croc got just a bite of my long hair, ripping some out right at the crown and sides of my skull. I rolled over and over, churning up beach sand as he chased me across the beach, the snapping jaws only inches from ending the battle. His evil red eyes glowed in the dim light of the night, and I could feel the heat of his rancid breath as he spit out blond hair. The massive jaws lined with razor-sharp teeth opened wide. He was now upon me.

The evil beast prepared to deliver the deathblow. Luckily for me, the string of Kalik cans entangling the croc's body snagged a piece of driftwood, momentarily distracting the creature long enough for me to regain my feet.

With his massive head turned far to the right, he began biting at the cans that ensnared him. That's when I made my move. Leaping through the air, I delivered a "Flying Superman Punch" to the croc's jaw before landing squarely on the beast's back. Now in full rear mount, I applied a figure-four leg hold around his belly and sank my fingers under the bony orbital ridges of both eye sockets, digging deep. I grasped the leather-covered supra-orbital ridges just above his eyeballs. With my death hold applied, it was now time to ride that son of a gun!

Just like an alligator, the croc began twirling and rolling in a death spiral. His enormous weight almost crushed me each time I was beneath the monster, but I clung to him for dear life. I knew he would eventually tire, and he did. That's when I released my grip on the eye sockets and began rubbing his belly with both hands, right at the spot where a human would have a bellybutton.

The sleeper technique worked! He began to quiver as if having a seizure, or maybe more like silent, hysterical laughter, before going limp, asleep. I didn't stop squeezing my figure-four leg triangle until I was absolutely certain he was out cold.

I pushed the sleeping reptile off me and hurriedly collected my equipment. Then I began to run for my boat. When I reached the water's edge, I glanced over my shoulder and to my surprise saw the croc running after me. He was gaining ground fast.

The sleeper hold should have lasted ten minutes at least. The clever reptile had played possum to get me off his back. He had never been asleep! Now I was in big trouble. No man can out swim a crocodile, and the tide had come up, putting a good 10 yards of water between the *Watermelon* and the beach. Running at top speed, I dropped all my gear on the beach and dove headfirst into the warm, shimmering water, swimming fast. I knew I would never make it to the boat, but I kept swimming faster than I had ever swum before, expecting at any moment to feel the crushing pain of those treacherous jaws.

To my amazement, I reached the boat and scrambled aboard the *Watermelon*. The crocodile of bull alligator was struggling in the gentle surf. The string of Kalik cans still entangling the creature had acted like an anchor and slowed him down.

Once again, my habit of over hydrating had been of great benefit to me. I would have perished if I had not emptied so many cans. I owe my life to that long string of empty Kalik Ale cans.

I pulled the anchor and drifted off the island and into the Gulf waters. The stubborn beast tracked me for a while, towing the 50-foot-long beer can anchor, but eventually he gave up and returned to his home. Only then, once out of danger, did I notice the bleeding and the deep gash on my left arm. As I began to lose consciousness I recall thinking to myself, *What a faker that mutant species was. How clever a crocodile of bull alligator can be!*

I made a silent vow:

If I survive this wound, never again will I believe a croc of bull.

I have lived my life following that tenet. I suggest you do the same, especially if you plan to read more of *The Secret Diary of Eddie Ocean.*

Chapter 2

THE WHATCHACALLIT TRIBE

NATIVE AMERICAN TRIBES OF FLORIDA

The "Invisible People" were the remnants of the once-mighty Calusa Indian Tribe. They had lived in seclusion for hundreds of years in a remote area of the Everglades near what is now the Big Cypress National Reserve in Southwest Florida.

The empire of the Calusa was once vast, extending from the Florida Keys north to Sarasota. They battled for territory and resources, reigning over their enemies, for hundreds of years until the late 1600s, when European settlers sold the Tequesta warriors muskets. The Calusa's reign came to an end as the "thunder sticks" instantly changed the balance of power, and the Tequesta Indians went on the warpath to destroy their enemy, the hated Calusa. Many Calusa fled to Cuba. Many more died of disease or in combat.

By 1700, only about 1000 of the Calusa people remained in Florida. They survived by retreating into the swamps and finding refuge on 144 acres of secluded land located on the southwest coast of Florida, just east of the Ten Thousand Island chain. The Calusa developed the ability to become "invisible." When outsiders approached, they vanished into the forest and swampland. Explorers, surveyors, and hostile tribes discovered well-maintained Calusa camps and lodges but were miffed at not being able to find any people. That's how the tribe became known as the "Invisible People."

After 200 years of living in total seclusion, each succeeding generation began to lose the magic of invisibility. In 1949, missionaries discovered a group of young Native Americans hiding near the main lodge of the Invisible People's village. The Native American children insisted that they were invisible and could not be seen as they squatted in the brush with their hands covering their eyes, trembling in fear. The missionaries could clearly see the frightened children and treated them kindly. Stealthily, the adult Invisibles watched the intruders, ready to attack them if necessary. When the Invisible People realized that the strangers had come in peace, they suddenly began appearing from behind trees and bushes and walking out of a misty fog. Mystically, magically, hundreds of people become visible and surrounded the startled missionaries, who cautiously greeted them.

Until 1949, the Invisible People had been living in hiding, unaware that their dreaded enemy, the Tequesta tribe, was nearly extinct. The Tequesta people had long ago been forcibly relocated to reservations in the southwest United States or absorbed into the social fabric of the white settlers in what is now Miami, Florida. But still, the Invisibles remained afraid to reveal their true identity as the Calusa tribe. The fear that the missionaries would reveal their location to Tequesta warriors remained.

The missionaries established a temporary camp near the Invisibles' village in order to study the indigenous Native Americans, and a close friendship between the two groups was quickly established. The missionaries were in the process of compiling a dictionary of Native American languages. In order to learn the native vocabulary, the whites were constantly pointing to objects and asking the Indians; "What do you call that?" The Indians caught on to the word game and would say the Indian word or name of the person, place, or thing in question.

To the Indians, the phrase "What do you call that?" sounded like one word, "whatchacallit." As a consequence, the first English word the Indians learned to speak was "whatchacallit." To them, this first communication was a great discovery. The Indians repeated the word "whatchacallit" while pointing to a subject and were thrilled when the white people responded with an English word. The people repeated "whatchacallit" often; they would smile and point at one another and for no good reason say, "Whatchacallit."

Those who called out, "Whatchacallit," were considered sophisticated, the enlightened elite. People began saying "Whatchacallit" when they were surprised or curious. They began saying "Whatchacallit" as a greeting. It was the newest fad, the pop culture; the English speakers might say it was hip or cool. The Indians would say it was whatchacallit!

Now that the people were no longer in hiding, the missionaries decided that calling them the Invisible People was not appropriate. They went to the chief and asked him by what name should his tribe be identified in *The Dictionary of Native American Languages*. The chief did not understand their question, so he immediately responded, "Whatchacallit?" As a result, in the year 1950, the missionaries documented the people living in the region of Big Cypress and the Ten Thousand Island chain as the Whatchacallit Indian tribe.

SUNDAY, JULY 22ND, 1973

The sea is an ever-changing chameleon. The black water on this moonless night waxed dark purple and then lightened to blue as the ocean was bathed in the early light of the dawn. The finicky sea finally settled into a brilliant shade of aquamarine as the sun rose higher in the sky. The Gulf of Mexico came to life as the nocturnal creatures went into hiding and the hungry daytime predators began to greet the dawn.

Unbeknownst to me at the time, but I would learn later, four young Whatchacallit fishermen had set off into the dark Gulf waters before sunrise paddling a pair of long, cedar, dugout canoes. The four young men had been fishing for over two hours now, and the sun was above the eastern horizon. They were a mile off the coast of the Florida peninsula skillfully casting large mesh nets from the canoes.

Below the boats, schools of baitfish were swimming rapidly in a tight, funnel-shaped circle. Larger predatory fish charged into the swirling vortex, feeding on the panicked baitfish. Through the clear water, the underwater feeding frenzy was visible to the men floating above the frantic piscatorial tornado. The men followed the moving bait pods, casting their large nets.

As the cast nets dropped down into the depths, they pulsed in the current like giant jellyfish, forming an inescapable dome of death around the fish. Under attack from above by the nets, the hapless prey dove deeper to escape, but the attack from below by the razor-toothed predators drove them back to the surface. It was a massacre.

A fishy, oily, slick began to spread over the calm surface. Soon terns, frigates, and sharks arrived to join the feast.

After each haul, the fishermen pulled open the fish-laden nets, spilling dozens of flip-flopping, multi-colored, silver-blue-green fish into the wooden hulls. To avoid the thrashing fish, the bare-foot young men straddled the boats, balancing with one foot on each gunwale while warily eyeing two large bull sharks that had joined the party and circled their canoes. Each time a catch was boated, the muscular, brown-skinned fishermen would toss their heads back. Their long, silky black hair whipped in the light breeze as they looked to the heavens and emitted wild, yelping howls, an ancient tradition to thank the gods for their generosity and to insure future good luck.

By 10:00 am, the young Whatchacallit warriors had already filled their boats. The days catch; a bounty of sardines, mullet, blue runners, mackerel, and an assortment of game fish would bring great praise from the tribal elders. The smiling young men called out loudly, "Whatchacallit!" before slapping one another hard on the shoulder.

To the east, the sun continued its ascent, rising above the Florida Everglades. Rays of sunlight now filtered deeper into the ocean depths. The surface water sparkled as if covered by a billion silver sequins. Beneath this translucent, glimmering surface the young men could now see all the way to the seabed. They paddled away from the feeding frenzy, toward the coastline. Occasionally one of the fishermen would point down into the depths and shout, "Whatchacallit," before diving overboard. The others laughed, joked, and pretended to toss the net over their companion as he resurfaced with a large conch.

The sea was calm, with only a gentle westerly breeze to provide some relief from the heat of the rising sun. The men made one last dive for conch and lobster before deciding to quit for the day. They had done very well and wanted to deliver their catch while it was still fresh.

Preparations were made to paddle back to shore. Checking his bearings, Jumping Jack, the leader of the group, looked westward toward the open Gulf waters. Something in the distance caught his eye. "Whatchallit!" he shouted as he pointed at a distant floating object. The others stood up to see. Something was adrift in the Gulf. The men could not identify the object. Was it a boat, or better yet some goods lost from a cargo ship? After a brief discussion the fishermen decided to load all the day's catch into one canoe so they could investigate the floating object. Black Skink, who was the youngest at fourteen years of age, was ordered to paddle home to deliver the fresh catch. The other three Indians went in the empty canoe to investigate the drifting object.

The three powerful warriors were excited as they paddled swiftly and with precision. Their synchronized strokes brought the canoe to full speed as they raced over the slick water. Within fifteen minutes the object was clearly visible: It was a boat. This discovery gave them pause. They had hoped for lost cargo. They slowed their pace and proceeded with caution. Pirates and just plain bad people sometimes passed through these straits. Those outsiders needed to be avoided if possible.

The odd-looking boat appeared to be adrift, unmanned and abandoned. Silently, cautiously, the young warriors approached the vessel. Paddling with one hand, they tightly gripped fish spears in the other. Suddenly, Full Moon began laughing.

"Be quiet!" Jumping Jack demanded with a hushed voice.

Full Moon's large, round face quivered and turned reddish brown as he attempted to silence his outburst.

From 100 yards out, details of the boat became visible. Suddenly, both Morning Wood and Full Moon began laughing. Muffled giggling became snorts and odd noises as the pair attempted to maintain silence. They could not control their hysteria. When they looked at one another, red faced and bug eyed, the immature young men bent forward, cramped over in an uncontrollable, painful delirium. Full

Moon was the first to completely lose control. He could not catch a breath without exhaling loud bursts of laughter. They both felt light-headed.

Realizing that his two childish friends had exposed them, the leader, Jumping Jack, called out to the small boat. "Hey! Hey! Hey! Anyone there?"

"What the heck *is* that?" asked Morning Wood.

"It's a giant dugout watermelon—a watermelon carved into a boat! Ahaaa! *Holy whatchacallit!*" roared Full Moon between gasps of laughter.

Jumping Jack was beside himself. "Shut up, you idiot! It's a wooden boat that's been painted like a watermelon!"

"Hey! Hey…we come aboard. You not mind." Jumping Jack spoke in broken English.

No one responded. The dugout canoe was brought up along side the watermelon boat and lashed with a hemp rope.

Jumping Jack noticed dried black blood on the red deck and then spotted a pair of legs protruding from under a tarp near the stern. He boarded the craft.

"Look! A body!" Jumping Jack exclaimed, gasping.

"Holy whatchacallit!" Morning Wood shouted. "The pirates must have got him!"

Jumping Jack pulled the tarp off the body and said, "Pirates would have tossed him over and stolen all this cargo. He must have died from some sort of accident."

"Look—his arm is ripped wide open," said Full Moon.

"Whatchacallit! His chest just moved!" said Jumping Jack. "He's still alive! Let's see if we can sail this watermelon boat home! Night Owl might be able to save this fellow! Hurry!"

Unconscious and near death, I was unaware of where the Indians were taking me. But as they say,

Any port in a storm

Chapter 3

THE VISION

FRIDAY, JULY 20ᵀᴴ, 1973

The evening of the day that I battled the croc, I lay seriously injured and adrift on the sea. Barely alive, I wondered if I could survive. I gazed up at the full moon, and the soft yellow light comforted me. Then a bright white light descended from the sky. The light had a human face and spoke to me.

"Come with me. Your ancestors are calling you," said the glowing face from within the light.

Strength returned to my legs, and I stood up. The descending light grew larger and enveloped me. I rose with it toward the sky. I looked down and saw the *Watermelon*. As I rose higher, my little boat appeared ever smaller as she drifted alone on the vast sea. I was sad to be leaving her behind, helpless and adrift. I recalled the promise I had made to the old Cuban sea captain, my vow to care for his little boat, and I felt guilty for leaving her behind. This was the first time that I understood the old man's intense love for the odd little boat. I, too, had come to love her.

Floating ever higher, I came to a place where it was daytime. I was in a green meadow, surrounded by vast plains that stretched to the base of enormous mountains in the distance. Every animal known to Mother Earth roamed or grazed across the land. Predators and prey all lived together. I felt total bliss and euphoria. No pain remained. I felt at peace and indescribably happy. All human needs, wants, and desires were satisfied in this wonderful place.

"This is the Meadow of Tranquility. Come quickly. The ancestors must speak with you. Your time is short," said the spirit.

Following the glowing face as it floated ahead of me, I realized that I wasn't walking; I, too, was floating forward. We arrived at the entrance of a giant teepee that rose high in the sky beneath a spectacular rainbow. The entrance to the teepee was through a waterfall, which washed us before entering. Inside, five old men and four old women sat in a row before me. The man to my left spoke with kindness, and I realized that these beings were not old men and women; they were ancient spirits.

"You have been chosen to serve us by helping our people on earth. We must now reveal to you your ancestors so that you understand why you have been chosen. See the people of the past. Then see your destiny—your future. See my life now!" said the ancient spirit.

In an instant, I saw the creation of the heavens and the universe by the great god Wanaka, the Father of all the spirits.

"Is that truly the Wanaka?" I asked the ancient, but he did not respond.

Then he spoke softly, but his voice could be heard across the universe. "Behold the universe."

The next ancient sitting in the circle spoke. It was a woman. "See now my life," said the second spirit. In an instant I saw the creation of Mother Earth.

"Behold my gift to mankind." This voice filled the universe and was beautiful to hear.

Are you the mother spirit? The spirit of Mother Earth?" I asked the old woman. She did not respond.

In rapid succession, each spirit revealed to me the origins of all forms of life—humans, animals, insects, and plants, and all of the wonders and power of nature: weather, tides, wind, and storms. The spirits that controlled everyday life on the earth were revealed to me, in the sky and throughout the heavens.

The spirit who sat to the far right spoke last. "See now the lives of your direct ancestors."

It was revealed that my great-great-grandfather had been a Viking explorer and warlord. My Norwegian ancestors had invaded and settled in the New World in the Great Lakes region that now encompasses parts of Canada and the Great Lakes region of the United Sates. But what was most surprising was when my mother's ancestors were revealed.

My mother's great-grandfather was Chief Pontiac of the Ottawa tribe. My great-grandfather had been chief of an Indian tribe in the area of Detroit, Michigan, which meant that my mother was an Indian princess. When she was still a child, the adults, including her parents, were forcibly relocated to reservations in North Dakota, and the children were taken by the government and forced to attend government-run "Indian Schools" under the direction of the Bureau of Indian Affairs. While in second grade, my mother was orphaned when both her parents died of heartbreak and despair at the North Dakota reservation. The next year, my mother was adopted by a family of Swedish immigrants and raised as a white child in Michigan and Ohio, never being taught her Native American heritage. I was shocked at this revelation. I realized that I was 50% Native American!

How can a man who is half Native American be born with fair skin and yellow hair? I wondered.

The spirit knew my thoughts and spoke: "The medicine of your ancestors, the Northmen, is very powerful. The Great Wanaka created you to resemble a Wasichu warrior from the North but to have the closeness and fondness for nature of your Native American ancestors."

My family had left Michigan and moved to Kentucky while I was still an infant. When I was a young boy, my mother had told me about having dreams of being an Indian princess. I thought her tales were part of the childhood games that we played in the woods of Kentucky. We built straw teepees and pretended to be Indians. These new revelations of my ancestry were hard to believe, but I knew they were true. It was clear to me that lying and deceitfulness did not exist in the Valley of Tranquility.

Again, the face in the light spoke.

"Your time here is over. You will follow me now." The light went back through the waterfall and out into the meadow.

"Where will we go now?" I asked.

"Follow me."

We traveled across the meadow to the foot of the mountains and then floated upward. It was cold, and snow fell upon us. There, on the side of the mountain, I saw a great lodge built from huge logs. We entered. Inside, seven very old men stood behind a long wooden table. They had beards and very long hair and wore horned helmets. The powerful men seemed to be seven feet tall and very broad.

"See now your Nordic ancestors." They spoke all at once and with one voice.

In a vision, I saw them sail to the New World long before human history was documented. They were great explorers and warriors, and I was surprised by their Spartan existence in such a harsh climate. Their barbaric and ruthless aggression against all enemies was disturbing—the more so since, apparently, these barbarians were my relatives!

"Now you must return to earth," said the face in the light.

"But I do not want to leave this place. It's wonderful here!" I complained.

The light went back up into the black sky and, although I did not want to go, I could not keep myself from following. Now the moon was visible again. The face in the light sensed my despair and spoke.

"When you return to earth, you will no longer ever be alone. Look over there." The face looked toward the north, and I did the same.

"That's the Big Dipper," I said.

"Yes, that is what humans call it, but it is the night council of the great spirits that you just attended. Those are your Nordic ancestors."

I counted the stars that form the shape of the dipper, and there were seven—one star for each spirit I had visited.

The face in the light now looked toward the equator and a different constellation.

"That is Orion, the great hunter of the night sky," I said.

"Yes, that is how humans identify the heavenly bodies, but the lights are the spirits of the night council in the Great Teepee—your Indian ancestors."

I counted the lights that formed Orion. Sure enough, there were seven main stars and two additional lights, planets, totaling nine. One for each spirit I had visited in the Great Teepee.

"You need only look to the heavens for guidance. The great spirits of two powerful constellations have chosen you to do service for them on earth."

I was confused. This was too much to comprehend.

This is such a realistic dream, I thought to myself.

"No! You are not dreaming. Now your time here is done." The spirit knew my thoughts!

SUNDAY, JULY 22ND, 1973

We descended rapidly, and I saw the *Watermelon* below. My body was lying on the deck in the stern. It was now morning, no longer night, and I saw three men with long black hair standing over my body. I felt a jolt of pain, and my whole body seemed to be on fire as my spirit reunited with my body. It was sad to return to the pain and hardships of the living. The excruciating, burning pain caused me to slip back into unconsciousness.

FRIDAY, JULY 27ᵀᴴ, 1973

When I awoke, my first recollection was of being a spirit in the night sky. Confused and not knowing where I was or what was happening to me, I thought I was dead. Above me, I saw the underside of a thatched, palm-frond roof. I noticed a coconut suspended from a rafter. A brown tube protruded from the bottom of the coconut. With my eyes I followed the tube from the coconut down to the bed where I lay. I was horrified to see that the tube went from a hole in the bottom of the coconut into a hole in my right forearm. I tried to sit up, wanting to rip the tube out of my arm, but I couldn't move.

I called out, but no sound left my cracked and swollen lips. I was dehydrated and too weak to speak or move. I just gazed wide-eyed at the hanging coconut, wondering what was happening to me. Shortly, the face of a young woman filled my view. She seemed to hover above me. Her large, clear brown eyes widened when she realized that I had awakened from my deep sleep. She smiled broadly. The brightness of her smile was surrealistically intense; it hurt my eyes. Framed by silky raven black hair, her entire face glowed within the misty hue. Her face floated like a helium balloon above me before disappearing. I closed my eyes, hoping that this new face in the light would take me back to the Meadow of Tranquility.

Was I dreaming, hallucinating, or meeting an angel at my death-bed? Had I actually traveled in an "out-of-body" experience to the Meadow of Tranquility? These thoughts and questions filled my mind. Then the beautiful apparition returned. This time a thin, very old man wearing a scary mask accompanied her. He was frightening. I closed my eyes, hoping he would go away, and I drifted again into unconsciousness.

SATURDAY, JULY 28TH, 1973

Night Owl, the medicine man of the Whatchacallit Indian tribe, doctored me back from the brink of death. I'm told that I slept for four days and was thought to be dead more than once. Night Owl had delivered the water of four coconuts into my bloodless body, a quantity of the natural plasma substitute and electrolytes that had never before been administered to one person.

Night Owl was a thin, old man with a heavily weathered face. He appeared to be wearing a wrinkled, dried leather mask, a mask that had been made by skinning a large lizard and tanning its hide in the sun. I sensed that his intense eyes could read my thoughts and see deep into my soul. I could hear him talking to me in a foreign language, but his lips didn't move, and he wasn't visibly speaking. The all-knowing eyes were clouded with cataracts. Most of his teeth were missing, and his long hair was as white as beach sand.

Night Owl had lived so long that all of his generation and most of the generation after him had already passed to the afterlife. It was well known that due to his knowledge of the earth's magic and its strong medicines, he had lived for more than 100 years. Some insisted he was over 200 years old.

I had many questions, but Night Owl communicated only in the ancient Calusa language. He was not good at interpreting my charades, and my animated antics seemed to annoy him.

Eventually a younger fellow, named Jumping Jack, came to translate for Night Owl. He spoke broken English, and I learned from him that the angel woman was real, not a hallucination. Her name was Little Hooters, the great-great-granddaughter of Night Owl. She had helped save my life but because of concern for her safety, she had been ordered to leave the medicine hut after I became conscious. The Whatchacallit people had good reason to distrust outsiders, especially white men, whom they called the Wasichu.

I was told that like her great-great-grandfather, Little Hooters was extremely intelligent and, at the age of twelve, she had become Night Owl's understudy and assistant. She had learned to speak fluent English and Spanish from missionaries living near the village. The missionaries were interested in learning ancient Native American medical remedies, customs, and language. Little Hooters taught them, and in exchange she and all the Whatchacallit children were taught English and Spanish at the mission.

She was proud when Night Owl asked her to continue as his understudy, learning the skills of the medicine man so that one day she could take his place. The missionaries encouraged Little Hooters to learn more from her great-great-grandfather, and to collect samples of the medicinal plants and minerals that he used, and to share those secrets with the white missionary doctors.

My translator/guard, Jumping Jack, did not appreciate my interest in Little Hooters. He remained suspicious of my intentions, especially when I told him that I hoped to see Little Hooters again. That made Jumping Jack angry and more suspicious and hostile toward me. He became annoyed whenever I asked a question concerning Little Hooters. Suddenly it dawned on me that Jumping Jack was *jealous*! He was obviously in love with Little Hooters!

Weeks later I learned that my instinct had been correct. Jumping Jack, along with five other young men, was courting Little Hooters. Jumping Jack was indeed jealous and unhappy at all the care and attention I had received from Little Hooters. He could not understand why the entire Whatchacallit tribe was so fascinated with me, a weak, helpless white man who had to be nursed back to life by a young woman and a frail old man.

Four days had now passed since my awakening. I was finally able to stand and walk on my own. I felt stronger with each passing day, and on the seventh day I left the medicine lodge. When I appeared in public outside the medicine hut, activity in the village came to a halt. Curious people stopped what they were doing and came over to get a good look at me, the yellow-haired Wasichu. My "shadow," Jumping Jack, waved them away, scolding them in their native tongue. Disappointed, the people reluctantly returned to their chores, mumbling, "Whatchacllit... whatchacallit."

I noticed Little Hooters in the distance, washing something by the river. She looked at me and smiled before mysteriously disappearing behind a misty fog. This was the first time I had seen her since my recovery. She was indeed beautiful.

Jumping Jack noticed me searching the riverbank with my eyes, looking for her.

"You know...Jumping Jack save you, fellow!" he said.

"I did not know it was you, Jumping Jack. I'm grateful to you. I owe you my life. I hope to repay you one day." I bowed to show him my gratitude.

My act of submissiveness and vow of loyalty seemed to diminish the uneasiness between us. Since my injury, I had lost twenty pounds and was both physically and mentally depleted. I knew Jumping Jack considered me an inferior weakling, and my kowtowing must have reaffirmed his opinion. Now he considered me even less of a threat, and that was fine with me.

Jumping Jack stood tall, chest puffed out, and slapped me hard on the shoulder. "Whatchacallit!"

The smack surprised me and hurt. I sensed that it was a good thing, not an insult; he seemed to be waiting for my response.

Ahh! I thought. *OK!* I slapped him hard on the shoulder, and he was pleased. This was the start of my friendship with Jumping Jack.

That evening the Indians made a large campfire and prepared a feast. I was introduced to the tribal leaders and put on display for the curious people. I learned that names given to the Whatchacallit people came at the moment of birth and were never prearranged. Things and events occurring in nature were taken as names to commemorate the moment of a child's birth and to appease and thank the gods.

Some names are self explanatory, like Running Deer. Others needed more explanation. I made a list of some of the more unusual tribal names.

Little Hooters was born on a night when two juvenile owls were loudly calling to one another.

The chief was Chief Thunder Butt. The chief was born a breech birth during a severe thunderstorm. Just as a loud clap of thunder shook the lodge, the first part of the chief's anatomy appeared, and it was his butt.

Jumping Jack was born at the fishing lodge as schools of jack crevalle were breaking the surface during a feeding frenzy.

Morning Wood arrived in the late morning just as the gatherers were returning to the farming lodge with a large supply of firewood.

Morning Wood's wife, Furry Beaver, was born in the hunters' village near the river's edge as a large, hairy beaver groomed himself on the opposite river bank.

The people of the Whatchacallit tribe greatly enjoyed gathering together and listening to the re-telling of the story of my rescue. Jumping Jack, Full Moon, and Morning Wood each took a turn describing the events. New details were added at each telling, making the story more exciting and dangerous each time. The chief would then insist that I tell my tale of being marooned on Crocodile Island and my battle with the giant croc of bull gator. The people listened, wide-eyed, and could be heard muttering, "Whatchacallit," especially when I described the attack and my fight with the monstrous beast. No one ever seemed to tire of my tale.

The next morning after my welcoming feast, I noticed that Swimming Mullet had cut his hair. It was trimmed shorter at the crown and sides of his head but left long at the back. The following day I noticed that several other young men had cut their hair in the same style, including Jumping Jack. I asked Jumping Jack about this new fad, and he said they were copying my hairstyle.

"That's not how my hair looks!" I said.

Confused, I walked over to a bucket of water and looked at my reflection in the water. Indeed, my hair was trimmed the same way.

"That damn croc of bull gator did this to me. He bit off a bunch of my hair!" I said.

"It looks good on a fellow," said Jumping Jack.

Soon nearly all the young men had cut their hair the same way. The elders frowned upon the new, non-traditional hairstyle. I did not like my new hairdo because it made me recall the evil eyes of the croc as it gave me the unwanted trim. It angered me to admit I was still afraid of that hideous mutant beast. I needed to conquer my fear; I had to return to Crocodile Island. I decided to return there and retrieve the equipment that I had abandoned on the beach. It was not right to leave my belongings with that devil beast. By going back, I would prove to myself that I was not a coward.

When I told Chief Thunder Butt that I planned on returning to Crocodile Island, he insisted that I choose three warriors to take with me. I agreed. I picked Jumping Jack, Full Moon, and Morning Wood, the three warriors who had rescued me.

Chief Thunder Butt said, "Before you leave, you must visit Weeping Willow. She will warn you in advance of the dangers that you will encounter on your journey. She sees into the future. If pre-warned, you can prepare yourself for every danger that you will face."

I found the witch's lodge. The woman was very old. She reminded me of a female version of Night Owl, the medicine man. Her lodge was full of odd-looking bones and skulls. She had drawers of herbs and powders and bottles of potions. She directed me to sit on a round, woven rug that was adorned with the images of many animals.

I sat but then stood up and began telling her of the dilemma that I faced, of being afraid to return to Crocodile Island but knowing it was something I needed to do. She ignored me. I realized that she did not understand me and did not speak English. She pointed at the mat, directing me to sit back down.

She threw a handful of animal vertebrae onto the rug in front of me and gasped, then began shaking her head. She gathered the bones and put them away. Then she called out to someone. A boy entered the room and sat cross-legged in front of me. He was waif-like, small, thin, and very pale. His strange, vacant stare made him appear very creepy. To me he seemed like an old man trapped inside the body of a sickly youngster.

"I Horny Owl...I here to translate," he said, speaking in broken English. My creepy hosts had a brief conversation in Whatchacallit.

"My grand say...beware the singing woman," said Horny Owl. "My grand say... the storm with the rain of stones will not harm you. My grand say...you can only defeat the dragon with fire."

"What you are saying to me? What you say has no meaning to me. I don't know what any of those statements mean," I protested. The boy just looked at me with a vacant, thousand-yard stare.

Next, the witch produced a glob of crystal-clear glass. I had seen one of those before. I knew that lightning striking and melting beach sand had formed the glass crystal.

Again she spoke to the boy, and then he said to me, "My grand say...you are not a white man...you are not an Indian man...you are both... or neither. My grand say you are hiding things from the people. Are you a friend of the people? My grand asks."

"Yes, I am a friend," I said.

The old, half-blind woman gazed into the crystal glass and went into a trance. Suddenly she began to laugh hysterically. She would not or could not stop laughing. Two minutes passed. Now five minutes. I could not stand it any longer! I didn't know what to do. I began to get up to leave, but I became concerned when it sounded like the old woman was choking and unable to breathe in between her fits of laughter. The boy sat staring at the glass and did nothing to help her.

I was concerned but did not know what to do. Finally I smacked her across her face, and she instantly came out of the trance and fainted.

The angry boy asked me, "Why you hit my grand?"

"It was for her own good. She was locked in some kind of a trance," I replied.

The boy revived the old woman, who sat up and immediately thanked me for bring her out of her laughing spell. This time she addressed me in English, but she had not spoken out loud. She was using some type of telepathy to communicate. I understood her. The boy could not hear her voice; it was only audible inside my head.

How did you know how to break the laughing spell? she asked, again in English and with telepathy.

I explained to the fortuneteller, "At first I did not know what to do. But then I remembered something my mother had taught me when I was a young man. My mother said, "When uncertain and unable to make a decision,

Always strike a happy medium!"

Chapter 4

MORNING WOOD'S MEAT

*****WARNING:** It has been brought to my attention that some people may find the following chapter offensive. Double entendre and hidden meanings or messages are solely in the demented mind of some readers, not the author!

WEDNESDAY, SEPTEMBER 26TH, 1973

The morning after the great feast, four hunters went deep into the forest in search of game. The tribe needed to replenish their depleted meat supply. The hunters shot two deer and one large hog with bow and arrow. After a short ceremony to honor the animals' spirits and to thank the gods for the successful hunt, the carcasses were field dressed, tied by the legs to long poles, and then carried back to the central lodge. The Indians had no means of refrigeration, so it was necessary to immediately butcher and either cook, salt, or dehydrate the meat.

Morning Wood took generous portions of the butchered pork and venison to the farming village where he lived. He distributed the food among the families living in the village. Morning Wood was courting Furry Beaver; a young woman who he hoped would soon become his wife. He selected a huge pork roast and presented it to Furry Beaver.

She was impressed by the size of the meat and gladly accepted the offering. Morning Wood asked Furry Beaver's mother, Angry Cur, "Could I cook dinner for you and your entire family tonight, Mama?"

"I don't know...*could* you?" Angry Cur spoke with an icy tone. And then she added, "Yes, you *may!*"

The Whatchacallit people have various ways to cook or dehydrate meats and fish. My favorite method is when they put the meat and vegetables into a large clay pot that has been soaked in water for at least two hours. The Indians call these pots "wet ovens." The saturated pot is placed directly onto red-hot coals until the meal is done. The result is the most tender, delicious roasted meat and vegetables that I have ever tasted. Early settlers in Miami learned this cooking method from the Tequesta Indians. To this day many white people buy clay pots called Romertopf and use the wet ovens to roast their meals.

Morning Wood chose to cook his prized pork roast in one of those soaked clay ovens. He noticed that Furry Beaver's oven was already wet and hot on the coals. He asked Furry Beaver if he could put his pork into her hot, wet oven, and she agreed. Normally this cooking method was foolproof because the wet clay pot keeps the meat moist by steaming it as it is roasting. Morning Wood, however, was a terrible cook and did not handle his meat well. His problem was that he was impatient and tried to hurry the process. He kept taking his meat out of the hot, wet oven, checking it, and then putting it back in. Furry Beaver became annoyed, but finally got him to relax, and he was able to finish the meat properly.

In the end, Furry Beaver admitted that Morning Wood's meat was perfect and the best pork she had ever experienced. In fact, Furry Beaver was so impressed that she accepted Morning Wood's proposal; she agreed to marry him.

MONDAY, AUGUST 21ST, 1973

I traveled to the farming lodge to ask Morning Wood to join my crew and me on our voyage to Crocodile Island. He told me about his romantic evening and of his wedding plans and said he had many preparations to make for the wedding ceremony and could not leave. He said that he would love to join my crew, but his future mother-in-law was already nagging him about the wedding details.

I told him I understood his situation and asked who he thought I should take in his stead. Morning Wood recommended Running Deer. Running Deer had proved to be an excellent shot with bow and arrow on the recent hunt. A skilled archer would be a great asset on our dangerous voyage, so I agreed to recruit Running Deer.

I wished Morning Wood good luck with his mother-in-law, Angry Cur, but before leaving I asked him, "Running Deer, I have learned that among the Indian people the woman of the house is boss...chief of the family's lodge. The man is only in charge when outside the lodge and when the couples are in public—or when danger threatens the family. Is all of this true?"

"Yes, the proof of a man's love for a Whatchacallit woman is his acceptance of the rule and domination by his mother-in-law." Morning Wood spoke slowly, with the voice of a doomed man.

"Well, you must really love Furry Beaver! Good luck with her mother, Angry Cur!"

He seemed to appreciate my empathy and pity.

"I must leave for the hunters' lodge to find Running Deer," I said.

"This is your lucky day, Sun Chaser Eddie Ocean. Running Deer is on sentry duty here at the farm."

"What is sentry duty?" I asked.

"Every night two hunters guard our crops against the grazers—rabbits, deer, gophers, skunks. They protect the crops, and it is easy pickings for the hunters," said Morning Wood.

Searching the perimeter of the large farm just as the sun was setting, I found Running Deer sitting in a tree. He signaled for me to get down and be quiet. He was looking down into the clearing below as he began to draw his bow and take aim. I stood up just enough to see over the bushes and spotted a large deer grazing in the distance. *Twang!* I saw the arrow arch high before descending from the sky toward the deer. Even at a distance of 100 yards, the deer heard the twang of the bowstring and lifted its head. The arrow descended from the sky and struck the deer just behind and below the left shoulder. The animal took one step and then fell to the ground dead, a clean kill.

"Whatchacallit! That was an amazing shot!" I shouted.

Running Deer did not respond. Instead he sat perched in the tree, head bowed, chanting something. His voice had a sad tone. When finished, he jumped down from his perch, and I realized he had been praying to the deer's spirit. We went to the deer, which lay on its side in a field of dill weed. It was a large female, a doe. As Running Deer field dressed the doe, I told him of my impending voyage and asked him to come with me.

Running Deer happily agreed to join my crew. Plans were made to depart in two days at 3:00 am. The early morning hour was chosen for good reason. First, the ten-hour trip to Crocodile Island would put our ETA at about 1:00 pm, giving us several hours before nightfall. I did not want to spend one minute on that island after sunset. Second, according to my tide chart, 3:00 am coincided with the beginning of the outgoing tide. The beginning of the outgoing tide was ideal for leaving port just as the end of the incoming tide is optimum for entering port. Sailors know that this strategy provides the deepest water with a favorable current.

We talked about the voyage as we carried the deer back to the farming lodge. When we arrived, a group of people had gathered outside a hut, and we heard a baby crying loudly.

"What is wrong with the baby?" asked Running Deer.

"Nothing at all! My granddaughter is a perfect, beautiful, newborn baby girl," said an elderly woman. We had arrived just after the moment of her birth.

"Let me present you with a gift. Here is a doe that I killed while it grazed in your dill weed patch," Running Deer said to the baby's mother. Running Deer laid the doe before the woman holding her newborn infant.

She spoke; "Thank you Running Deer! You shot the doe in our dill weed patch, so I will name my baby girl 'Dill Doe' to honor the animal's spirit and to please the gods!"

"I'm sure that Dill Doe will be very popular and have an exciting life," said Running Deer.

As the sun was setting, Running Deer and I walked from the farming village. I asked him what he had been saying in the tree after he shot the deer, and he told me that after a kill, the animal's spirit is thanked for its sacrifice to the people.

That brought another truism to my mind:

Kill them with kindness.

Running Deer returned to his sentry position, and I left to go to the fishing village to find Jumping Jack.

Chapter 5

SUN CHASER EDDIE OCEAN

Jumping Jack and I went to the *Watermelon* to unload in preparation for our voyage to Crocodile Island. It was dark when we summoned several dog soldiers to carry twenty cases of Kalik Ale to the central meeting lodge. Four cases of the ale were left onboard so that my crew could remain well hydrated while at sea. All of the straw hats and carved monkey heads were also offloaded and carried to the central lodge.

People were worried that if we returned to Crocodile Island the great, mutant croc of bull alligator would attack us. To ease the tension, Chief Thunder Butt announced that the tribe would hold a war feast to bring luck to the three brave Whatchacallit warriors and also me, the brave Wasichu. A large fire was built in front of the grand meeting lodge, and people began arriving from all three outlying Whatchacallit villages. The hunters, the fishermen, and the farmers each had a seating area reserved for their congregation.

Due to their royal and sedentary lifestyle, the chief and his wife were the only obese members I saw among the tribe. Thunder Butt stood 5'8" and tipped the scale at 300 pounds, and his wife, Hog Snapper, was 5' 2" and at least 250. The rotund couple sat atop a heavily reinforced, elevated platform built from sturdy bamboo.

They sat facing the fire pit near the front entrance of the grand meeting lodge. Four dog soldiers, which is what warriors in training are called, stood guard near the chief. Fifty Whatchacallit warriors stood encircling the fire pit.

Many wet clay ovens could be seen heating on top of the coals, and above the red-hot coals a spit holding a large hog was turned slowly with a hand crank. People began chanting, "Hey! Hey! Hey! Hey!" as the food was served.

It is good manners in the Whatchacallit people's culture to show one's approval of a meal by belching loudly and often. Loud flatulence is considered even higher praise. Chief Thunder Butt's flatulence techniques were the envy of all the men and boys of the tribe. His reputation for long duration, extreme volume, and his pitch-altering skills were legendary. Hog Snapper exemplified impeccable etiquette as well. She was a model for all the women and girls to follow and was highly respected for her long and loud belching skills. She was the epitome of a gracious hostess.

The people took feasting seriously. While eating it was rude to talk. The slurping and sounds of mastication were exaggerated to show their great appreciation. The explosive farting and burping increased as bellies became stuffed. The warriors encircling the fire had been fed in advance at a private ceremony, and they stood guard over the gluttonous people. I noticed that the chief's bodyguards had moved several feet away from his platform. The gaseous noises being emitted by the chief and Hog Snapper were truly impressive. For everyone's safety, I was glad that the chief was not seated close to the open fire.

People emptied their plates and sprawled out with swollen bellies, blissfully burping and farting. Then, with all the food consumed, a squealing sound equivalent to the gas being released from the stretched openings of a hundred party balloons came from Chief Thunder Butt. The chief's final gaseous salutation started as a long, high-pitched sound, then went through the mid-ranges before ending with a deep bass tone, a rumbling that shook the bamboo platform. The four highly disciplined dog soldiers guarding the chief swooned momentarily, gasping for air.

As if celebrating the grand finale at a fireworks display, the people stood and cheered. "Hey! Hey! Hey! Hail Chief Thunder Butt!"

People reveled in the chief's impressive expression of satisfaction. The hunters, fishermen, farmers, and cooks, all those who had made the feast possible, were greatly honored by the chief's spectacular gaseous expulsion. Then with great effort, Thunder Butt rose from his chair. Close to his chest, he held a scepter adorned with eagle feathers.

"Weeping Willow has asked to speak to the people," announced the chief.

Weeping Willow walked to the speaking spot, a small mound of crushed shells near the fire pit. The people she passed cowered and trembled in fear, hoping that she would not judge them or place a curse on their families.

I feared that the old witch was going to denounce me to the people and have me punished for striking her across the face.

"The Wasichu (white man) sitting among us is not what he has been pretending to be!" she spoke loudly. The nearly blind woman turned in my direction.

"The spirits have revealed to me this man's true identity." She pointed her wrinkled, crooked index finger at me. She was frightening.

"He pretends to be weak, but he is hiding great medicine." Warriors stepped toward me and raised their spears. My friend Jumping Jack led them. He gazed at me, an expression of confusion spreading across his face.

"He is not just Wasichu. He also has the blood of the Indian people—the Indian people of the north. His mother was from the Ottawas—a powerful war tribe that fought the Wasichus for many summers." She pointed toward the north.

"But he also has the blood of the white Nordic barbarians who first sailed to our lands! Yes! He has the blood of the Viking barbarians! The Northmen who attacked our people for over a hundred years." She pointed the crooked finger up, toward the Big Dipper.

The chief stood, pumping his scepter into the air as he spoke. "A wolf, even if tamed, cannot be trusted to live among the sheep. How can we trust this man? Will he not turn on our peaceful people like the wolf upon the sheep? Like the Viking barbarian whose blood flows in his veins, he cannot be trusted! Viking blood is strong medicine! No man can deny his own blood! Like the wolf, no man can resist his primal nature!"

Weeping Willow spoke loudly. "The great spirits said to me that they have visited with this Wasichu, Eddie Ocean. They revealed to me in a vision that he is not to be feared. He is our friend. They said that they have given this half-breed a mission. They have commanded him to help our people unite and make peace with our enemies, to spread peace, not war. They have chosen him because he has our Indian blood as well as the blood of our enemies, the Wasichu barbarians." Once again she directed the dreaded finger at me.

"In my vision another deception was revealed! Our Indian ancestors call this man 'Sun Chaser,' his Native American name, not Eddie Ocean." She stared at me, scrutinizing me for what seemed like an eternity. I could not tell if she was defending me or prosecuting me.

The chief finally broke the silence. "Let Sun Chaser speak! What do you have to say, Sun Chaser...Eddie Ocean...whoever you are? Explain your deceptions! Explain your secrets!"

I looked at Jumping Jack standing with the other forty-nine armed warriors. He nodded, encouraging me to speak. I gathered my courage and spoke, sensing that my life might depend on my explanation. "My entire life, I did not know...."

The angry chief interrupted me. "Speak up louder! Like an Indian man, like a warrior!"

"I said, my entire life, I did not know that I had Indian blood. I did not know I had an Indian name. I did not know I had Viking blood. I did not learn any of these things until my spirit traveled to the Meadow of Tranquility, when I lay in my boat near death. That was the night before I was brought to your village."

Many people gasped in disbelief. Many considered me to be blasphemous for saying that I had visited the Valley of Tranquility.

I continued; "Yes, it is true that the ancient spirits called for me and spoke to me when I lingered near death. The ancients, both Wasichu and Indian, are no longer enemies in the Meadow of Tranquility. Spirits from all corners of the earth live together in harmony. Animals that are enemies on earth walk together in the meadow. Many wonders were revealed to me. What Weeping Willow said is true. I have been commanded by the ancient spirits who reside in the heavens to do service for them on earth."

I pointed at the seven main stars and two planets in the southern sky that comprise the Orion constellation.

"Those lights are the spirits of nine Native American ancients taking council in the Great Teepee, where I met them."

Then I pointed north to the Big Dipper. "Those are the seven ancients of the Norsemen at council in the grand lodge, where I met them.

"See! Look to the west of the Big Dipper. The sky is full of the spirits of the ancients. They are conducting their nightly councils in the Meadow of Tranquility. In the afterlife all the spirits of nature and the heavens are at peace and in harmony with one another. No pain, wants, or needs exist, only joy and happiness! It is beautiful there!" I said.

Some of the people began to protest what they perceived as my heresy. "Liar! He lies!"

Weeping Willow spoke on my behalf. "He is telling the truth. He would not know these wisdoms if the ancients had not spoken to him."

The chief called me to his throne. He raised his scepter above my head. I prepared myself for the blow.

"I decree in the name of the great spirits that from this day forward you will be known to our people as 'Sun Chaser Eddie Ocean.' People will know that you symbolize the peaceful uniting of the Wasichu ancients with the ancients of the Indian people."

He touched the scepter to my forehead. "I now bestow upon you all tribal rights. You are the adopted son of the Whatchacallit nation. You will join the brotherhood of the Whatchacallit warriors. You will live among the Whatchacallit dog soldiers until you are ready!"

The chief seemed to be waiting for me to speak. I did not know how to respond to such an honor. Finally, I remembered the cargo from the *Watermelon*.

"This is a great honor, Chief! Please accept my gift to you and the people, an expression of my gratitude."

I walked to the front porch of the central meeting lodge; there a large tarp covered my cargo. I pulled it off, revealing the stack of Kalik ale, the straw hats, and carved coconut monkey heads.

"Hey! Hey! Hey! Ya!"

The entire tribe chanted and ran to the gift pile. There were enough hats for everyone. The chief stuck a large turkey feather in his straw hat, and the children snatched up the carved monkey heads. People began drinking ale. Some spit it out, and others grimaced but kept drinking the strange brew.

Chief Thunder Butt squatted low and let out a thunderous fart. Then he stood straight, pumping his scepter skyward with one hand and raised a can of Kalik ale in the other as he called out. "Bitterroot water! Yum! Yum!"

It became apparent to me that the Whatchacallit people had no concept of adult beverages because they were giving Kalik to young children. Inebriated people began acting foolish.

Suddenly, I heard loud drumming, and the fifty warriors ringing the fire began circling and dancing with a hopping motion. The disciplined warriors had not partaken in the scramble to the gift pile, so they did not wear hats. Their long hair, trimmed, shaped, and layered like mine, was tossed wildly about as each dancing warrior passed by me. They poked my chest just above my heart with their spears. The tips pricked my chest, inflicting small, painful bloody holes in my skin. I stood my ground as blood dripped down my breast. After a couple of passes, my blood coated every spear tip; then they pulled me into the ring of dancers. I tried to duplicate the war dance ritual, hopping and spinning, but was out of rhythm with the others. I saw women and men laughing, Little Hooters was grinning from ear to ear. I felt embarrassed.

Sensing my discomfort, Chief Thunder Butt said, "Let Sun Chaser Eddie Ocean show us the war dance of the Wasichu warriors."

I did not know how to dance to the *um-pa* thumping sound of the drums. The beat brought to mind an Oktoberfest party and the chicken dance that I had learned when I was attending college in Philadelphia. I formed my hands in the shape of a chicken's beak and, with the beat of the drums, simulated four pecking motions. Then I flapped my arms like chicken wings four times to the beat. My wings became a tail as I put my hands behind my back, fingers pointing up like feathers, and wiggled downward. I rose back up, clapping to the beat.

The people roared with laughter. Dancing must be the universal language because an old man whom I knew to be named Dancing Bird ran over to join me. He was a natural at dancing the ridiculous chicken dance, and his big, floppy straw hat was the perfect attire for such foolishness. Now the people rolled around on the ground, laughing so hard that their overstuffed bellies ached. I think the bitterroot water had begun playing a role as well, and the festivities grew ever wilder.

"That is a good dance! Wasichu men must fight like angry roosters!" said the chief.

"Show us another!"

Disco dancing had become popular in my homeport, Miami. I had learned a few dance moves at clubs on South Beach, so it was the only other dance that came to mind. The Whatchacallit drummers were using large bass drums with deerskin covers, and smaller, bongo-sized percussion instruments as well. The beat that they played was *BAM...bam...bam...bam...BAM...bam...bam... bam.* I needed a disco beat. To demonstrate, I struck the drums with a different beat, a bit of a Latin rhythm. The skilled drummers picked up the rhythm instantly and began playing a beat better suited for disco.

I went back to the fire pit and grabbed old man Dancing Bird and began parrying and spinning him around. The warriors were fascinated. To them this dance looked like two men sparring, a dance that simulated battle. Charging forward, parrying to the side, grasping the opponent and spinning to avoid his counterattack, and then retreating to prepare for the next offensive move. All fifty warriors paired up and started disco dancing. To them these movements were like a karate fighter practicing his kata.

I stopped dancing and gazed at them in amazement. This was a sight to behold! Fifty muscular warriors in loincloths with styled, layered haircuts disco dancing to the beat of Gloria Estefan! It reminded me of the Monster, a bar at 400 Front Street in Key West, where I occasionally delivered my Kalik ale.

Clouds of dust rose above the fire pit as the warriors danced and the people cheered wildly. The dance progressed as the dancers improvised and added athletic movements. They were transforming my disco dance into a fusion of disco, West Coast swing dance, and a violent mosh pit slam dance. They tossed each other into the air, slid between legs, and hopped high over each other's head. For me, disco would never look the same.

The chief and Hog Snapper were ecstatic—they loved the show! Hog got up and pulled Thunder Butt out of his chair, demanding that he dance with her. They tried to grasp hands, but their combined girth made that physically impossible, so they just spun like tops, circling each other. The two out-of-control behemoths spun and hopped around until the bamboo platform collapsed beneath their enormous weight. Even that did not stop them. They crashed trough the rubble like a pair of rhinos and continued dancing toward the fire pit.

I saw them dancing one in front of the other, and it reminded me of a conga line dance. I took Hog Snapper's hands and placed them on the chief's hips as she followed him around. Then I got behind Hog and placed my hands on her ample hips. People caught on to the conga line. Little Hooters latched on to me, and soon I looked back to see the longest conga line I had ever witnessed! I needed a break, but the nonsense continued for hours.

When I went to my sitting spot to rest, I noticed a pile of various items occupying my seat.

"What's this?" I asked.

A man answered my question. "It is Whatchacallit custom to give gift when receive gift. This is gift—gift for you from the people."

I looked through the pile and found exquisitely crafted jewelry, fine leather goods made from soft deer hide, and artwork of carved bone and ironwood.

"These things are very valuable. You could trade items like this in Miami for much wampum! Crocodile Island is just a hop and a skip from Miami. Do you want me to do a trade for you in Miami after I leave Crocodile Island?" I asked.

My idea was presented to the chief, and he liked the plan. He had my gifts carried to the *Watermelon* and promised to have men and women bring more of the beautiful handcrafted items in the morning.

"How will I know whose items I'm trading?" I asked.

"It does not matter. All the goods that you bring home from Miami will be divided among the people," said the chief.

Eventually people went home or passed out in grassy areas around the central meeting lodge. It was late when I began walking to my boat, and I was nearly home when a young boy jumped out of the bushes. He looked about nine years old.

"Eddie Ocean, I must warn you! My friends are going to steal your funny-looking boat tonight," said the boy.

The boy told me that a group of his young friends planned to sail the *Watermelon* to an out island, two or three miles from the coast. They said they were going to have their own private party and drink the four cases of Kalik ale that I had left onboard.

"I think it is bad medicine to steal, even if it's just for fun," said the boy.

"Thanks for the warning, kid. I just might have a little fun of my own tonight."

Jumping Jack was walking home toward the fishing village when I stopped him and told him what I had learned. We both sprinted to the *Watermelon*. She was still docked; nobody had come to steal her so far. I went into the cabin, got a sack of flour, and began dusting myself from head to toe.

"Here, powder yourself. We will teach these young pranksters a lesson!" I said to Jumping Jack.

He poured flour over his head and torso.

"Use the bosun's chair to hoist yourself up to that port side spreader," I said as I tied a double-looped bowline, slipped my legs into the loops, and then hoisted myself up to the starboard spreader.

Now we both hung by ropes, suspended high above the deck. The white flour made us look like ghosts. Shortly, we heard whispering, and then we saw boys creeping from the bushes toward the boat. When they were onboard, their attention was directed down at the cuddy cabin, probably wondering if it was occupied.

Jumping Jack began swinging through the air above them. He shouted, "Hoka hey! Hoka hey!" the war cries of the Indian warrior.

Surprised, all nine boys looked up to see two ghosts hovering in the night sky above them. At least one of the future warriors wet his loincloth!

I pushed off from the mast and began swinging as well. Then I poured the remaining flour down on the boys as they scrambled about the deck in terror. Now, with white heads and faces, they were scaring each other. Two jumped overboard and swam to shore. The others crashed into one another as they raced toward the gangplank, screaming. Their saucer-sized eyes revealed their terror.

"Hoka hey! We are the guardian ghosts of the *Watermelon*! Hoka hey!" Jumping Jack thundered.

We could hear the boys crashing through the underbrush, some of them crying as they ran home.

As it turned out, the boy who ratted on his friends had unwittingly saved their lives. Early that morning, gale force winds and fifteen-foot seas surprised the people. Everyone hunkered down in shelters. If the inexperienced youngsters had sailed the *Watermelon*, she surely would have gone down in the violent storm, taking all nine boys with her to a briny grave.

My young informant was named White Cloud. Children began calling him *White Rat!* He felt guilt and shame for squealing on his friends. Seeing his sadness, I gathered the children together and told them that the great spirits in the sky must have called on White Cloud to stop the boys from taking my boat.

"When called upon by the spirits, a man has no choice but to obey. This I know. White Cloud had no choice—he had to stop you from taking the boat!" I told them. "You all should be grateful to White Cloud. He saved your lives!"

That made White Cloud feel better, and his friends stopped tormenting him. They gave him newfound respect.

The lesson that was learned that night is that

A snitch in time saved nine!

Chapter 6

THE KISSING PLACE

THURSDAY, SEPTEMBER 27ᵀᴴ, 1973

I was making a final check onboard the *Watermelon* in preparation for our voyage to Crocodile Island when I heard someone calling to me from the shore.

"Sun Chaser Eddie Ocean, are you home?" It was Little Hummingbird, Little Hooters' best friend. I walked down the gangplank to the beach. "Hello, Little Hummer!"

She smiled. She liked when I abbreviated her name.

"What brings you out here?" I asked.

"I come on behalf of Little Hooters. She wants to meet you tonight before you sail away to Crocodile Island."

This request surprised me. Other than the one time in the conga line, Little Hooters had been shunning me and keeping her distance. She rarely made eye contact with me. Although at least five Whatchacallit men were courting her, everyone knew that Little Hooters was committed to marry Jumping Jack.

"I would like that!" I said. My face must have been aglow as I grinned from ear to ear.

"Go to the Kissing Point under the great pine trees after sunset." She also had a broad smile and giggled as she began to walk away.

I was about to thank her but hesitated, wondering if I had heard her correctly. "Did you say *the Kissing Point*?" I called out. She stopped, turned around, laughed, and then nodded her head.

I must admit something that I have not yet revealed about the first time that I saw Little Hooters, as I lay near death and only semiconscious. I cannot say why, but even then, I knew that I loved her.

How can you love someone you don't even know? I pondered. *Can a grown man be love-struck, like an adolescent?* These questions made me reminisce about my first childhood romance.

As a young boy, I considered girls to be annoying. They were strange creatures, but there was one girl who was an exception. She was different because she did not enjoy dressing up in high heels, having tea parties, or playing house with the other girls. She would rather throw a baseball or go fishing with the boys. She was much less annoying than any of the other girls whom I knew growing up in Kentucky. Her name was Maggie Darling.

When I was around twelve years old, something strange happened. Almost overnight I became interested in girls. Suddenly, I began feeling attracted to the mysterious creatures, and Maggie Darling stole my heart that summer.

Maggie Darling no longer looked like a child. For the first time I noticed how pretty she was with her long auburn hair, freckles, and that beautiful smile that rarely left her face. She was fun to be around—she was a tomboy. She could run faster than most of the boys, including me. She climbed trees and swung in the branches as well as us boys. Maggie was also smart and very kind to every person, even the mean kids. She enjoyed helping very old people and would listen to their stories for hours when she had the time. She loved animals and had a big, sloppy basset hound that followed her everywhere; she spoiled that dog rotten.

The summer before my thirteenth birthday, Maggie became my first girlfriend. I kissed her one afternoon while we were sitting in an oak tree. All that summer we played catch, climbed trees, built forts, and swam or fished in Pippin's Pond. I began to feel a strange longing, an inner sickness when I was not around Maggie Darling. I would walk in the street outside her house, hoping she might come out; if she did not, then I would feel even sicker. I eventually got over the sickness when my family moved to Pennsylvania. Although I wondered about her from time to time, I never saw Maggie Darling again, and I had never met another girl like her until now.

It embarrassed me that at the age of twenty-two, that old childish lovesickness had returned. When I saw Little Hooters and she would not speak with me, I felt that sickness creeping back into my chest.

~

Kissing Point is a beautiful outcropping of limestone that forms an elevated, rocky point extending over a deep tidal basin. Giant Australian pine trees provide a shady canopy over the secluded spot. On windy nights, the trees sing as the wind whistles through the long, thin pine needles. Someone had split a long log and set it upon two stumps to provide a comfortable bench for sitting. In the daytime, people picnicked and fished there; at night couples, both young and old, came to share romantic moments and to view the night sky.

I arrived at about 9:00 pm. It was dark. I didn't see anyone. I sat alone on the ground with my back to the trunk of a large pine tree and looked up through the branches at the night sky. Directly above me, I saw Orion and imagined the ancients holding council in the Great Teepee in the Valley of Tranquility. As I gazed up, I visualized their faces just as I had seen them in my vision, and I no longer felt alone.

The cooing of an owl interrupted my thoughts. I looked high into the tree to find the bird.

"Whoo...Whoo! Whoo...Whoo!"

It sounded like a small owl, probably a young one. I stood up and circled the tree, looking into the branches. I wanted to spot it. Then

I heard laughter coming from a bush and another call. "Whoo… Whoo are you looking for?"

Little Hooters walked out from behind the bush. "You are a funny man, Sun Chaser Eddie Ocean. Any of the Whatchacallit people would have seen me in one heartbeat. Tee-hee!" she giggled.

"Well, you're a real riot too, Little Hooters!" I said sarcastically.

"Shhhh." She put a finger to her lips. She had a concerned expression as she turned toward a hedgerow and pointed with a signaling motion.

I walked to her side and whispered, "What is it, a panther?" I reached for the knife in the sheath on my belt.

Again she put her finger to her lips. "Shhhh," She tilted her head sideways, listening intently. Then she leaned into me, pretending to kiss my cheek, but only whispered, "There are children hiding over there. They come here to spy on the lovers."

That phrase "the lovers" did not go unnoticed, and I think my heart skipped a beat. I whispered, "I have an idea. Follow my lead. Pretend to be afraid."

I pointed into the tree branches above us and, in a high-pitched voice, I shouted, "Help us, Great One! There are white ghosts descending upon us! Help us!" Little Hooters began screaming, and then crouched down, covering her head with her arms.

Then in a very deep voice, I shouted, "Hoka hey! We are the ghost guardians of the *Watermelon* boat! We are searching the forest for the naughty children who want to steal our boat!"

The hedgerow began shaking like it had just been struck by a whirlwind. Children went running and screaming from the bushes. They ran toward the village. I was sure they would not return here tonight.

We both laughed. Then Little Hooters hugged me.

"All the people are talking about the ghosts living in the *Watermelon*. Some say it is a hoax; some say they are real…especially the children. Jumping Jack told me what you two did! I laugh until my ribs hurt whenever I think about it! That was a good lesson you gave to those little trouble-makers."

"Speaking of Jumping Jack...he is my friend, and I know he is courting you. Why did you want to meet with me here tonight?" I felt uncomfortable, but I did not resist her embrace.

"I have known Jumping Jack my whole life. I love him like a brother. Our families want to match us together, so for a long time now, I've felt that marrying him was inevitable...my only destiny. Then you came here. Now I feel differently," she said.

"But until tonight, you wouldn't even talk to me, wouldn't even look at me," I said.

"I avoided you because I was afraid of my desire to be with you. Whatchacallit women may not look upon any Wasichu man. It is forbidden. But that taboo changed at the war feast when Chief Thunder Butt decreed that you are now a Whatchcallit Warrior." She gazed into my eyes and squeezed me tight. I resisted my urge to kiss her.

"Some of the people don't accept me as one of their tribe. To them I'm the Wasichu. What makes you think that your family will accept me?" I asked.

"The greatest desire of every Whatchacallit child is to please their parents. Yesterday, I greatly disappointed my mother when I told her I did not want to marry Jumping Jack. She is not speaking to me." Little Hooters looked down at the ground, shook her head, and began to cry.

I put an arm around her shoulders to console her, and we stood in silence for a moment. Then she continued. "I had a big argument with my mother when I asked for permission to look upon you. She told the elders she did not want me to look upon you. Then the all the elder women had a big argument among themselves. Some women said it did not matter what the chief declared, I still could not look upon you because you are part Wasichu!"

She stepped away from me and began waving her arms to reenact the drama of the arguing women. "Everyone was yelling all at once!

They went before the twelve wise men—the high council—and continued to argue! I followed them to the high council, and I told the council that I wanted to look upon you because you are now one of our people. The council sent us away and had a very long discussion before calling us back into the meeting lodge.

"They decided that by the law, Chief Thunder Butt's decree was final and could not be challenged. I now have permission from the elders to look upon you, but my family is still angry with me." She looked up, searching my face for my reaction; I did not know what to say.

She broke the awkward silence. "So I now come to look upon you, Sun Chaser Eddie Ocean!" she smiled and gazed into my eyes. Her smile faded, and she furrowed her brow. "Why do you look unhappy? A woman knows when a man likes her, I know you desire me," Little Hooters said defiantly.

I was impressed at how fearless and forthright this young woman was. Most of the Whatchacallit women were introverted and shy. I doubted that any of them would tell a man she had come to look upon him.

I said, "You misunderstand me. This is great news! My heart aches for you, but what about Jumping Jack? He is my friend. Jumping Jack saved my life! I fear he will not take your decision well."

"We must not worry about the future. Our destinies will find us. I just needed to have you know how I feel before you sail away to Crocodile Island. I could not bear the possibility of never seeing you again without having expressed my feelings for you." She squeezed me tighter.

"Our destinies will find us...yes...I was told that once before," I said.

Her statement put me at ease; it took the pressure off me to think that our destiny was out of our hands. Who were we to control destiny? I decided not to tell her about my vision of sorrow. Destiny would take care of our future. I put my arm around her waist, and we both looked up at the moon above. Then I kissed her for the first time. Her lips tasted like honey, and her breath had a sweet scent.

"You taste like candy," I said and gazed into her large brown eyes. She was the most beautiful woman I had ever seen.

She pulled some honeysuckle flowers from her pocket and ate one. "Now you know a secret—a Whatchacallit woman's trick." She offered me a flower to eat; it tasted good.

We spent the night talking. I felt as if I had known Little Hooters my entire life. It was as if she had always been with me somehow, hidden somewhere in my heart. I think she felt the same way about me.

"Isn't it time for you to sail?" she asked.

I had lost track of time. I was completely captivated by Little Hooters' physical and spiritual beauty. Nothing else in the world seemed to matter to me anymore.

"You're right! It's almost 3:00 am! I can't believe how fast the time went by! Walk me to my boat," I said.

"No. Jumping Jack will be there. Please don't tell him about my feelings for you. I need to talk with him alone—in person. I will talk to him when you return."

We kissed again, and it was hard to let go of her hand; it was hard to leave her.

As I walked away, I knew that no matter what our destinies might be, I would never forget this special night. An old truism came to mind:

A minute on the lips, a lifetime in the heart

Chapter 7

ATTACK OF THE PIRATES

FRIDAY, SEPTEMBER 28TH, 1973

I boarded the *Watermelon* at 2:55 am. Jumping Jack, Full Moon, and Running Deer were sleeping on deck near the bow of the boat. The moonless night was very dark, the air hot and humid, with only a light breeze. The high tide was just beginning to recede. A wisp of wind brought a pleasant odor from the forest, and I breathed in deeply to fill my nostrils with the scent of night-blooming jasmine. The sweet fragrance of the flowers reminded me of Little Hooters. Starting the diesel engine, I looked toward Kissing Point and remembered kissing her. The sound of the boat's motor woke my three crewmates.

Jumping Jack was the first to spring to his feet and greet me. "Hey, hey, hey, Captain!"

"The tide is running strong. Let's cast off the lines, men." I motored forward, dead slow. "Jumping Jack, go to the bowsprit and spot the channel for me."

Holding on to the standing rigging, Jumping Jack walked out on the bowsprit. He was reading the water and directing me with hand signals so that I could keep the boat in the middle of the narrow, shallow channel. Once we were clear and into open water, he came back onto the deck. The full moon was starting to rise behind us in the eastern sky, and it provided some light to navigate. A favorable westerly breeze came up as we moved away from land.

"Hoist the mainsail," I ordered.

I shut down the engine, and we continued onward under sail. Only the sound of water splashing against the hull and the wind in the sheet could be heard.

"Why don't you fellows get some more sleep? I don't think I can rest yet. You can relieve me at sunrise," I said.

I was still too excited to sleep; thoughts of Little Hooters dominated my mind. Looking astern, I saw the full moon, which now was much higher in the sky and directly above the Whatchacallit villages.

Is Little Hooters sleeping, or like me is she too excited to sleep? Might she also be gazing up at the beautiful moonrise, thinking of me? She was the only thing I could think about.

The wind picked up, and we gained speed. After reading my compass, I set my course on a bearing of 257 degrees. We were sailing southwest. Two hours passed, and the full moon was now directly overhead. The sea glistened in the soft light. I spotted a land mass off the starboard bow and identified it on my chart. It was Great Pine Island. The island was covered with many large Australian pine trees, some well over 100 feet tall. As we approached, I heard the wind singing through the pine needles and once again was reminded of my embrace with Little Hooters under the trees at the Kissing Point.

The island was directly off my starboard beam when I heard the voice of a young woman singing. The beautiful song was coming from the shoreline; the voice accompanied the whisper of the wind through the pines. I adjusted my course a few degrees so that the boat would pass closer to the island. I wanted to hear the words that the woman sang. The song was beautiful and mesmerizing. Suddenly, Weeping Willow's voice was loud in my head.

"Beware the singing woman!" she shouted.

Startled, I did what I should have been doing all along; I looked ahead of the boat to where I was sailing. Less than twenty yards directly ahead, white water foamed at the surface, illuminated by the light of the moon. The disturbance was water breaking over coral reef hidden just inches below the surface. I yanked the wheel hard to port, and the *Watermelon* heeled over, tossing my crew from their bunks. I heard a scraping sound as the sharp coral marred the wooden hull of the *Watermelon*. Narrowly escaping disaster, we regained deep water.

"Hey, hey, hey! What's happening?" the men called to me as they scrambled to the gunwale and looked over the side at the hull.

"I almost hit a reef!" I said.

In the bright moonlight we all looked at the foaming reef. I knew they were wondering why I had not spotted the danger well in advance. The skeleton ribs of many wrecked ships were visible rising out of the water along the reef. Embarrassed, I did not tell the others about the singing woman. Instead I made up an excuse for my poor seamanship. "I must have been falling asleep at the wheel," I lied.

"You rest now. We will take over, Captain," said Jumping Jack.

"OK. Keep her on a heading of 257 degrees. That will run us right into Crocodile Island." I went below deck to my bedroll and hammock.

Before I even had a chance to lie down, I heard the men jabbering excitedly. I went back up to see what was going on. They were pointing back toward the island.

"It's nothing!" said Jumping Jack.

"No! I just saw it again. Look! There it is!" Running Deer pointed into the darkness.

Clouds had passed in front of the moon, making the night turn suddenly dark, but as the moon came clear once again, it bathed the sea in light. Outside the reef, two long racing sculls were clearly visible. Several men furiously rowed the boats in our direction.

"Whatchacallit! Who are those fellows?" Full Moon shouted out excitedly.

"Don't want to find out!" I said as I took the wheel, started the engine, and put the throttle full, wide, open. The chase was on!

The *Watermelon* is very seaworthy, but she was not built for speed.

"They're gaining on us, Captain! Do you want me to shoot them?" asked Running Deer.

"No, save your arrows. Don't know if they are after us or just taking the same course as we are on." That was the second error in judgment that I made that night.

"They are within twenty-five yards!" someone said.

Now they were close enough that we could see their faces illuminated in the moonlight. In the bow of the lead boat, a tall, thin man stood upright as all the others rowed. He had a very long, thin, weather-beaten face with a wicked-looking scar that traversed from the left side of his forehead down across to his right jawbone. He began twirling a rope above his head like a cowboy with a lasso. Then he flung something toward us. It was a grappling hook!

It landed on the deck and then snapped backward toward the stern. The hooks dug into the wooden transom, and the exhausted men stopped rowing and began producing weapons. We were now towing both boats behind us, and it was clear that these were men of bad intent!

"I think it's time to open fire, Running Deer!" I yelled.

He stood and took aim with his bow but was forced to duck for cover when the tall fellow fired an ancient, black powder musket.

Pow!

Jumping Jack ran toward the transom with his knife drawn in an attempt to cut the towline but had to dive for cover to avoid the shot. The musket ball sizzled past my left ear and hit the mast. I crouched low, still steering the boat, and saw the pirate pull his other musket and take aim at my head.

Twang!

An arrow flew barely a foot above my head and amazingly went right down the bore of the pirate's musket just as he pulled the trigger.

Pop

The gun made an odd sound, and with a bright flash and a cloud of smoke exploded in the pirate's hand. He fell backward into his boat, screaming in pain. The other pirates began climbing over their injured mate and attempted to board the *Watermelon*.

A stout, heavily tattooed pirate leaped into the *Watermelon*, holding a long dagger in his right hand. With a downward motion he stabbed at Jumping Jack. The agile warrior stepped forward to meet the attack. With his left hand, Jumping Jack grabbed the wrist holding the dagger. He parried by stepping to the left and under the raised arm as he grabbed the attacker's waist with his right arm.

Jumping Jack and the pirate spun around twice before Jumping Jack dropped down low to gain leverage. The pirate's expression revealed his surprise at Jumping Jack's quick footwork. Then, all in one spinning motion, Jumping Jack hoisted the guy high overhead and tossed him overboard. The screaming pirate looked like he was flying as he soared headfirst, kicking his legs and waving his arms. I could not believe how far the guy flew through the air before landing with a splash.

"I discoed that fellow!" Jumping Jack grinned as he yelled to us.

The other pirates were now in our midst. Running Deer could not shoot for fear of hitting a friendly. Full Moon was rolling around on the deck, wrestling one of the intruders, while Jumping Jack fought in the stern, trying to keep more pirates from boarding. A guy came at me with a dagger, and I threw a side kick, knocking the pirate into the drink. Then I pulled my own knife to cut the towrope.

Just as Jumping Jack pushed a pirate back into the longboat, I cut the towrope. The *Watermelon* was still under full throttle, and we began to get some separation from the drifting pirate boats. Angry pirates who had been unable to board us cursed and threw their daggers at us as we motored away. One frustrated pirate gabbed a long wooden oar and threw it at me. I was busy steering the boat and did not see it coming

Bonk!

The heavy oar bounced off my head and dazed me for an instant. A welt began to rise on the back of my head as Running Deer fired an arrow into the bow of the lead boat. The warning shot convinced the pirates to cease their attack.

Jumping Jack sat down on the gunwale to watch Full Moon wrestle the only remaining pirate.

"Do you want me to help him?" asked Running Deer.

"No! He getting flabby. Full Moon needs a good workout! Enjoy the show! Get that fellow, Full Moon, get him!" Jumping Jack yelled and laughed.

The pair rolled over and over across the deck before crashing against the transom. My evasive maneuver to avoid the coral reef must have shaken a carved coconut from its hiding place because it had been bouncing around the deck ever since. Full Moon grabbed the screaming monkey head sculpture and bashed the pirate in the side of his head.

"Hoka hey! He's out cold! Good one, Full Moon! That's using the old coconut!" said Jumping Jack, who laughed at his own joke.

Full Moon was not happy. He was pissed.

"Thanks for the help, friend! That fella could'a killed me! Plus he smells like a skunk!" whined Full Moon.

"What will we do with the stinky fella?" asked Running Deer.

"Tie him up. When we go to Miami we can turn him over to the authorities," I said.

We tied the unconscious pirate's hands and feet and put him below deck. He reeked of body odor and dead fish. When he came to, he began yelling and demanded to be let go. I closed the hatch to muffle his cries.

"I guess I won't be getting any sleep today with that fellow onboard! I might as well eat something," I said and began getting some salted fish.

"Look, we have more company today!" Running Deer called out as he pointed into the water at the bow.

Four dolphins were swimming fast and darting back and forth in our bow wake. They began leaping high in the air and making excited squeaking sounds. Jumping Jack began calling back to them by imitating the high-pitched sound. This made the dolphins even more excited, and they jumped very close to the boat.

"They say that they will show us where the dorado are. They want us to follow them," said Jumping Jack.

"You're joking, right?" I asked.

"No joking! Follow them!" he insisted.

Reluctantly, I veered off course to follow them as they swam fast just below the surface and angled off to our port side. After a few minutes, they once again began leaping high in the air and chirping excitedly.

"They say the dorado are here!" said Jumping Jack.

The experienced fishermen began unraveling hand lines. The fishing lines had bright yellow-feathered lures tied to the end. The trolling lures were tossed into the water behind the boat, and within minutes both men were hooked up.

"I got one!" A hooked fish jumped high into the air, shaking violently in an attempt to spit out the hook. Full Moon began to pull in the fish. Then the other one began leaping, hooked by Jumping Jack's lure.

Both fish were landed and flip-flopped about the deck. They were iridescent with the colors of a bright, beautiful, neon rainbow. I know the species as "dolphin fish" or "mahimahi," but the Indians called them "dorado."

The four dolphins surfaced near the boat. Each had a dorado in its mouth. They waggled their heads proudly as they displayed their catch.

"Thank you for finding the fish!" Full Moon called to them, and then he began making the chirping sounds.

The dolphin made one final leap, squeaking excitedly, and then they were gone.

"You don't expect me to believe that you fellas can talk to dolphins, do you?" I waited for them to laugh at me for falling for their scam, but they just looked at me like I was crazy.

"Of course we can. We can communicate with many animals. Can't you?" asked Jumping Jack. He was dead serious!

"Well, I guess I never really tried," I said, still waiting for them to get their laugh at my expense.

The dorado were filleted and grilled on a small cast iron hibachi that I keep onboard the *Watermelon*.

"This sure beats the dried, salted fish!" I said as I washed down the delicious grilled fish with a Kalik. There was more fish than we could eat.

"This fish won't keep in the heat. See if our stinky guest, the ornery pirate, wants to eat," I said.

Full Moon opened the hatch, and it smelled like a skunk had sprayed our cuddy cabin.

"Oh, that's gross! Give him the fish and close up the hatch!" I said. Another truism came to mind. Long ago, I learned that:

Fish and guests both stink after three days!

Chapter 8

RETURN TO CROCODILE ISLAND

"**L**and ahoy!"

I'm sure that my face turned a whiter shade of pale when I saw the coastline of Crocodile Island in the distance. The mutant crocodile bull alligator was almost certainly lying in wait for me there. My crew seemed nervous as well. They had heard the tale of my epic battle with the devil beast at least a hundred times by now.

The pirate was brought on deck and untied. I made him an offer. "When we leave this island, you may sail with us and face the authorities in Miami, or you can stay here and deal with a giant croc that inhabits this place."

The pirate looked at the forest beyond the beach. The lush forest contained many fruit trees and banana plants. If not for the croc-a-bull gator inhabiting the island, I would have considered it a tropical paradise.

"I'm a wanted man in America. I see there is much food and fresh water here. I will stay on this island, but you must leave me a weapon," said the pirate.

"We will return your dagger, but you will not get any weapons until we are ready to depart," I said. I did not trust the shifty-eyed pirate.

I sailed the *Watermelon* along the shoreline until I spotted my old campsite. We dropped anchor in shallow water just off the beach and waded ashore. Running Deer took his bow and arrows; the other two Indians were armed with fish spears, and the pirate grabbed the long wooden oar to use for self-defense.

Onshore, I found my dive mask, snorkel, and spear gun strewn along the beach where I had dropped them months ago as I fled from the giant croc. I also found what was left of my dive fins. The flipper part of both fins had been chewed off, and the rubber shoe part was full of large puncture holes. I collected all my belongings and put them into the boat. My tent had been ripped to shreds. Long, ragged strips of canvas hung from the poles. It was a total loss.

Full Moon and Jumping Jack began collecting fruit in the forest, and the pirate, armed with the long oar, began scouting out his new home. Running Deer told me that he wanted to see if he could track down the giant croc. Despite my opposition, he jogged off into the forest armed with his bow and arrows. "I'll be back in less than two hours!" he said.

I brought a large canvas tarp ashore for the pirate to use as a tent. "I suggest that at night you sleep up in the trees," I said to him as I dropped the tarp at his feet. He looked at the dagger I had taken from him; it was tucked into my waistband.

"Just give me back my dagger, and I'll be fine," he said.

"I told you, you'll get it when we are safely aboard ship and sailing away from this island."

Two hours passed, and Running Deer had not returned. We became concerned. After three hours we decided that we should search for him before it became dark. We began following a stream that led deep into the forest.

Because I didn't trust the pirate, I told him to leave the oar on the beach, and I made him lead us so I could keep a close watch on him. I certainly did not trust leaving that thief alone with the boat. With my spear gun in hand and Full Moon and Jumping Jack carrying the long fish spears, we cautiously proceeded deeper into the forest.

"Stay together!" I said.

"This place very bad!" said Jumping Jack.

Under the heavy canopy of the dense forest, the light was dim. Away from the stream, the forest was an impenetrable thicket of trees, brush, and thick vines. It was much cooler here than on the beach and oddly quiet. I wondered why we heard no birds, no sound of wildlife at all—only the sound of the babbling stream.

"Running Deer! Where are you?" we called out every few minutes.

Finally we heard the sound of his voice up ahead. "Go back! Get off the island!" In the distance there was a bend in the stream, and we could see Running Deer frantically waving his arms as he called out the warning. He was perched high aloft in a banyan tree.

"The croc is here! Go away—fast!" I had never seen such a look of fear on Running Deer's face. It was unnerving.

"We no leave Running Deer!" said Jumping Jack as he started jogging toward the banyan tree. He raised his spear, and Full Moon and I followed, but the pirate did not. As we passed beside the pirate, he snatched the dagger from my waistband and pointed it at me threateningly.

"Don't try it! I'm a surgeon!" he warned me.

Having no time to waste, I did not confront him but instead kept running, following Jumping Jack. The pirate retreated back downstream toward the beach.

When we reached the bend in the stream, we spotted the giant croc chewing on the trunk of the huge banyan tree. Like an angry beaver, he was chewing through the tree trunk. The beast was enraged and hissing like a dragon. I saw arrows sticking in his head and body where Running Deer had shot him. His eyes glowed red with rage and hatred. Running Deer looked terrified as he helplessly gazed down at the monster from his lofty perch.

"Holy whatchacallit!" yelled Jumping Jack when he saw the size of the croc. He had never seen such a hideous beast.

I knew the croc would attack us. I called out to Running Deer, "Running Deer, when that thing comes after us, get down. Run back to the boat! We can outrun him on land, but stay out of the water."

"Hoka hey!" Jumping Jack ran forward like a javelin thrower and hurled his spear. It struck the giant croc in the back but bounced off the beast's armored spine. The preoccupied croc whacked the tree trunk with his powerful tail, causing the whole tree to shake. Running Deer clung to its branches for dear life. Surprised by the blow from the spear, the enraged beast turned its attention toward us. It bellowed and then charged us with quick, short, choppy steps.

"Run for the boat!" I screamed in horror.

We all ran. I was on the heels of Jumping Jack, and Full Moon, who was a slower runner, trailed behind, barely keeping ahead of the enraged croc. We splashed along the bank of the stream, running for our lives.

Full Moon runs for his life!

We sprinted out of the forest and onto the beach. To my relief, the croc had lost ground and was lagging behind Full Moon. We knew we would make it safely to the boat until we all came to a sudden stop, not believing what we were seeing. In horror we stood in the middle of the beach, watching the pirate sail away in the *Watermelon*!

"Whatchacallit!" Jumping Jack gasped.

"Come back here, you dirty, filthy son-of-a-gun!" I screamed!

The pirate turned and laughed as the boat moved away from shore. Then he must have experienced a glimmer of compassion. "Here's a going-away present, mate! Maybe some fool will rescue you guys!" The pirate hurled my flare gun onto the beach.

I heard the roar of the croc behind us. We had to act fast. We spread out to form a semi-circle, and this seemed to confuse the croc. He stopped charging and examined us with those dreadful, glowing red eyes, maybe trying to pick the weak link among us. Just as the croc started to charge Full Moon, Running Deer emerged from the forest, sprinting at full speed. He ran up behind the croc and leaped onto its back.

"Hoka hey!" he yelled and began stabbing the beast in the head with his knife.

The croc began spinning in a circle like a dog chasing its tail.

"Hoka hey!" yelled Jumping Jack as he also leaped onto the croc's back.

The pair rode the reptile like a bucking bronco as they stabbed at him with their knives. The long, sharp knives seemed to only annoy the giant bull crocodile. Full Moon gathered his courage and dove onto its tail, attempting to stop the croc from spinning. The beast was too powerful and flipped him head-over-heels high into the air. He landed with a *thud* on his back in the soft sand and gasped for air.

The croc had had enough of the unwelcome riders and went into that familiar, rolling death spiral. Over and over it rolled along the beach. The weight of the monster was too great, and the Indians had to let go and jump off the beast or be crushed. The croc had grown even bigger and heavier since I had last seen him.

Running to the water's edge, I retrieved the flare gun. When I turned back toward the battle, I saw Full Moon lying on the beach helpless and gasping for air. He was unable to move—the wind had been knocked out of him.

The croc charged my defenseless friend as he tried to crawl away. Full Moon felt the long wooden oar lying in the soft sand under his knee. He grabbed it and rolled onto his back just as the croc was upon him. With massive jaws wide enough to swallow Full Moon in one bite, the hulking croc towered above Full Moon and hesitated. He seemed to be anticipating the savory meal before him.

Full Moon's torso was now in the jaws of the croc. Everyone watched in horror, waiting for Full Moon to be killed. But Full Moon thrust the oar vertically into the cavernous mouth just as the croc snapped his jaws shut! The sturdy oar broke in half, but the broken pieces of wood prevented the croc from fully closing his mouth. Running Deer and Jumping Jack took this opportunity to run to Full Moon's rescue. They snatched their friend from the jaws of death and dragged him to safety. The broken oar was now tightly wedged in the croc's mouth and holding it open.

Paralyzed with fear, I could not move until the voice of Weeping Willow once again filled my head: "Defeat the dragon with fire!"

Once again Weeping Willow's voice had come to my rescue. The state of shock left me, and I realized I was holding something in my right hand: It was the flare gun.

The ancient spirits had promised to guide and protect me. My courage returned, and I ran toward the croc, taking aim and firing. The flare went into the croc's open mouth and down his gullet just an instant before the oar completely shattered under the enormous pressure of the beast's bite.

The croc did not seem to enjoy his red-hot appetizer! He exhaled with a loud hiss. Smoke and fire billowed from his mouth and nostrils as he roared in pain. The fire-breathing dragon began running toward me! I thought the end was at hand, but to my amazement the croc ran right past me and into the water, where he submerged and disappeared.

"Hoka hey! Do you think you killed him?" asked Full Moon.

"I doubt it. I think that croc is immortal! He is *el Diablo*!" I said.

We all sat down on the sandy beach, exhausted.

"We are marooned on this island! What will we do now?" asked Running Deer.

"We must build a raft. We can use the tarp as a sail," I said.

We began collecting bamboo poles and cut wood from trees. We gathered long strands of vines to use as rope. I walked south on the beach to collect driftwood and noticed something in the distance, far down the beach.

"A sail!" I called out to the others.

We ran down the beach toward the sail. It was the *Watermelon*! The boat was listing to port, and the sail fluttered in the wind. The pirate had run her aground on a sandbar.

The four of us swam out and boarded the boat. The pirate was below deck, trying to get the engine started, and had not seen us coming. Enraged, we all grabbed a piece of him, ready to tear him apart.

"Hey wait! Let me explain!" he cried.

"If you had not helped us by throwing the flare gun ashore, I would kill you right now!" I fumed.

"I planned to send a rescue party for you, but the engine stopped running. I couldn't steer with the sail...I don't know how to sail," said the pirate.

"You must be the lamest pirate in the Caribbean! You can't fight, and you can't even sail a boat!" I mocked him.

"I swear, I was going to send you help!" insisted the pirate.

"I don't believe you, but I will return your favor: I'll leave you here with the flare gun. Now get off my boat before I change my mind!" I demanded.

It would be at least an hour before the incoming tide could lift the *Watermelon* off the sandbar. To pass the time, we relaxed on deck hydrating our bodies with Kalik ale and watching the forlorn pirate wandering around aimlessly on the beach. I felt sorry for the lame pirate but knew he had chosen his own destiny by living his life of crime.

I tallied our losses for the day. In the battle with the croc we had been very fortunate, but we had lost all of Running Deer's arrows, the flare gun, and the large, wooden oar.

I guess one might say

We won the battle but lost the oar!

Chapter 9

GOING TO MIAMI

FRIDAY, OCTOBER 26ᵀᴴ, 1973

We sailed for three days and three nights before passing under the seven-mile bridge just south of Key Marathon. Here we left the Gulf of Mexico and entered the open Atlantic Ocean. Crocodile Island was now over 300 miles behind our wake. On the afternoon of the fourth day, we were twelve miles due east of Key Largo and sailing swiftly north with the assistance of the Gulf Stream. A frightened frigate bird landed atop our mast. The large bird was visibly exhausted.

In the Whatchacallit language, Jumping Jack began speaking softly to the bird. Jumping Jack's voice seemed to soothe the frigate. It answered Jumping Jack by making a series of clicking and chirping sounds and continued resting atop the mast for about ten minutes before letting out a loud squawk and then flying off toward Key Largo.

After the bird was gone, Full Moon and Jumping Jack began jabbering excitedly in the Whatchacallit tongue. They kept looking toward the southeast horizon and, with flared nostrils, sniffed the breeze. They were worried about something.

"What's the matter?" I asked as I steered the boat.

"Aponivi! Aponivi! The bird was frightened of the aponivi!" said Jumping Jack.

"What's an aponivi?"

"Whatchacallit! I don't know the Wasichu word," said Jumping Jack. He began waving his arms and moving his hands in giant wave-like motions, playing a game of charades.

"Is it a storm? No? Bigger? Is it a hurricane?" I guessed.

"Yes! That's it! A hurricane—out there!" said Jumping Jack as he pointed nervously toward the southeast horizon.

"It looks cloudy, like a front—that's all. Why do you think there is a hurricane?" I asked.

"The frigate bird warned us," said Full Moon.

"Come on, not again! First dolphins and now birds are talking to you guys? Well, don't worry. We are only about four hours away from the port of Miami. The weather seems fine, and with the way the wind is picking up we might make Miami ahead of schedule," I said as I trimmed the sail.

I was wrong. Thirty minutes later the sky to the southeast began to look ominous. A fast moving wall of thunderheads with many lightning strikes was coming toward us. Large swells began rolling in and lifting the boat up, and then we surfed back down the waves.

Running Deer, who lived in the hunting village and was not a seafaring man, became seasick and was not of much help. The rest of us began preparing the boat. Things began crashing about below deck, so we tied down our cargo of Native American crafts as best we could. Then we reefed the sail as the wind velocity increased and began howling through the standing rigging.

Running Deer began vomiting, and he literally turned green. He could no longer stand upright, so he went below deck before we battened down the hatch. Stinging, heavy rain started pounding us, and the waves grew even larger. Ten-foot waves began to crest and break onto the boat. We were in danger of being swept overboard by the crashing waves. Clinging to the wheel, I steered the boat as best I could.

With the sail reefed in, I had limited control. No fuel was left to power the engine, and we were at the mercy of the wind and waves. The lack of control put us in danger of broaching, entering a death roll, and capsizing.

I recognized the fear in the eyes of both Jumping Jack and Full Moon. I knew they saw the same look in my eyes. I wished I had a sea anchor onboard so that I could heave to and ride out the storm. Then I had an idea.

"Jumping Jack, take the helm!" I yelled over the roar of the wind.

With difficulty, I struggled to get to the bow of the boat. Once there, I untied the heavy anchor from the anchor line and located a large twenty-gallon bucket. Using a sturdy bowline knot, I attached the anchor line to the bucket's handle. Hail the size of golf balls began bouncing off the deck and pummeling us. One stone hit my head, and I felt a welt rising from my scalp. To keep from getting killed, I took a smaller, five-gallon bucket and put it on my head. The handle went under my chin, and the bucket functioned as a helmet. Now I could only see to the front of me below my chest.

As the hail bounced off the bucket, I held the rope just below my chest and tested the bowline knot for strength before tossing the large bucket off the bow. I paid out 200 feet of rope before tying the line to the bow cleat. I had improvised a sea anchor from the bucket.

"Jumping Jack, heave to!" I called out.

Jumping Jack turned the boat directly into the wind, and soon the anchor rope attached to the twenty-gallon bucket became taut; the drag of the sea anchor/bucket kept the boat under control, with the bow facing into the wind and waves. This was a much safer position for riding out the storm, and we were less likely to capsize.

Hail pounded the bucket protecting my head, and the waves grew ever higher. *We're not going to make it!* I thought.

Then the voice of Weeping Willow was once again in my head. I remembered what she had told me: "The storm with the rain of stones will not harm you!"

Instantly, fear left me, and I began to laugh. With the knowledge that we would survive this storm, I began to enjoy the mighty power of the wind and sea. I walked out onto the bowsprit and shouted into the raging wind, "You are beautiful! No matter how angry, no matter how loud you howl, you are still our beautiful mother ocean."

With the sea anchor now controlling the position of the boat, Jumping Jack abandoned the steering wheel and went below deck to escape the painful barrage of hail. From beneath my bucket, I began humming Wagner's symphony *Der Fliegende Hollander, The Flying Dutchman,* as I stood on the bowsprit waving my arms like an orchestra conductor. I began singing.

"DAH...DAH...DAH...DAAAHHH...DAH! DAH...DAH... DAH...DAAHHH...DAH! DAH...DAH...DAH...DAH!"

Wagner had been inspired to write his opera following a stormy ocean crossing in 1839, and now I made his masterpiece my own as I conducted his symphony being played by Mother Nature.

Below deck, my Indian friends peered out of the forward porthole, watching me as I waved my arms like a lunatic with the bucket covering my head. I am sure they were worried that I had lost my mind.

"Sun Chaser Eddie Ocean, get inside before you are killed!" cried Full Moon.

I didn't heed his advice. Frantically waving my arms, I pointed out each lightning strike with my invisible conductor's wand. My string section was the sound of the wind through the sailboat's rigging, the booms of thunder provided a percussion section, and the sizzle of the breaking waves was my cymbals.

"You are a powerful, magnificent storm!"

I did not fear the storm because I trusted Weeping Willow's wisdom, and I trusted the ancient spirits who had promised to guide and protect me.

Fortunately, the eye of the hurricane was well out to sea, moving toward the northeast Atlantic and away from us. The hailstorm suddenly ceased and was replaced by gentle rainfall. The sound of my mighty orchestra was fading in the distance, reduced to a high school band marching off toward the horizon. I took the bucket off my head and hopped down from the bowsprit. The deck was slippery and full of large hailstones. I began collecting the ice with the bucket, and when my friends emerged from below, I asked them to help. We all collected ice, and then we took a case of Kalik ale and put the cans in the ice buckets.

"Sun Chaser Eddie Ocean, you are very brave man! Why you no fear the ocean storm?" asked Jumping Jack.

"I was terrified!" I said.

Jumping Jack had a puzzled look on his face as he pondered my admission. "That mean, Sun Chaser Eddie Ocean, you not brave fellow, you just crazy fellow."

"I've been told that before! Let's celebrate and do some hydrating! I give thanks to the gods." I was still yelling; my eardrums were ringing from the loud drumming of the hailstones on my bucketed head. My crew and I sat down on the cold deck and enjoyed the cold brew.

"I haven't had an ice-cold brewski for a long time!" I shouted.

Even Running Deer, who was not fond of ale, enjoyed the cold Kalik. "This bitterroot water much better when cold!" said Running Deer.

The wind died down to a stiff, fresh breeze, and the angry sea began to calm down. We pulled in the sea anchor and set sail for the port of Miami.

"Land ahoy!" I was the first to spot the skyline of downtown Miami.

The *Watermelon* entered Government Cut, and we sailed her past Fisher Island and Dodge Island. At Dodge Island several enormous cruise ships were preparing to disembark from the port. Onboard the ships and high above us, crowds of people ran to the railing to greet us. They were waving and calling to us with adult beverages in hand. My odd-looking boat, the *Watermelon*, crewed by three Native Americans wearing loincloths, was a big hit with the inebriated tourists. Some pretty, young girls threw leis to us, and we put them around our necks. Once past Dodge Island we turned north and sailed under the MacArthur Causeway.

At 3:00 pm on Friday, October 26th, 1973 I docked the *Watermelon* at a concrete seawall just north of the Miami *Herald* Newspaper building. Reporters in the building had seen us sail past, and they gathered in front of large plate glass windows to get a better look. Some observed us with binoculars as we waved to them. When they saw us dock nearby, many came outside to greet us.

One reporter asked us, "Who is your corporate sponsor? Is this a Halloween promotion? What products are you pushing?"

"We have come from our home in the Big Cypress to trade the goods and the crafts of the Whatchacallit tribe. We are looking for Slick Willie's Trading Post," I told him.

A young woman with a notepad pointed at Jumping Jack and asked me, "Are you saying that they are really Native Americans and that this watermelon boat is not a prop—all these oddball props are not designed for a Halloween promotion of some kind?"

"That's right. We have been sailing for four days. Now we are taking our goods to Slick Willie's, the trading post on 15th Street."

We began unloading our cargo onto the asphalt pier.

"Ouch! The pavement is burning my feet!" I cried out in pain as I hopped around on the hot asphalt.

My barefoot Indian friends stood on the hot, blacktopped pier unaffected. The soles of their feet were tougher than leather. They laughed as I danced back to the boat.

"Here—put these on, tenderfoot!" Jumping Jack mocked me by doing a little jig; then he handed me the chewed-off dive fins. The croc had reduced them to a pair of rubber shoes full of holes. They looked silly, but they did protect my feet from the hot pavement.

A crowd had formed. They wanted to get a look at the oddball sailors and the ridiculous-looking boat. The large crowd made my three Indian friends nervous. They kept looking at the crowd and then into the distance as if worried about something lurking out there.

Running Deer spoke to the woman reporter. "Do you know where the Tequesta camp is located?" he asked.

Now I realized why my friends were fearful. They thought that the Tequesta Indians of Miami (who had been extinct since 1770) were lurking among the crowd or on the streets nearby. Ever since the first musket attack took place in 1711, stories of the brutal slaughter of the Calusa people have been passed down from generation to generation. My Whatchacallit Indian friends, remnants of the ancient Calusa tribe, still lived in fear of the Tequesta.

The woman reporter mistakenly thought that Running Deer was asking for directions to the *town* of Tequesta, Florida and told Running Deer, "To get to Tequesta you will have to sail over 100 miles farther north and enter the Jupiter Inlet. You will know you are there when you see a red lighthouse—the Jupiter Lighthouse.'

The news that the Tequesta tribe had relocated 100 miles to the north lightened my friends' spirits and brought wide smiles to their faces.

"Lucky for them! Lucky for the Tequesta warriors! Lucky they leave Miami before we come," said Full Moon as he pounded his chest with his fist. The reporter did not understand what he was talking about and looked at him with a puzzled expression.

We collected six eight-foot-long 2x4 pieces of scrap lumber scattered about on the pier, and with small tarps made three pony drags. We loaded our goods into the pony drags and began walking down 15th Street toward the trading post. The sight of three Indians walking down the street in Miami, pulling pony drags loaded with

Native American crafts drew a lot of attention. Many people began following us. The reporter asked a lot of questions and was busy scribbling on her note pad as she walked with us. Her photographer friend took some pictures of our group.

Eventually we found Slick Willie's Trading Post at 172 N.E. 15th Street and went inside. I explained to Slick Willie that we did not want to make a cash deal because the Indians had no use for paper money. He agreed to barter. In trade he agreed to give us a bill of credit that we could use to purchase goods from his store. I haggled with the cheap son-of-a-gun, but he was offering only pennies on the dollar, not the full value of our beautiful and finely crafted merchandise.

A tourist who was visiting Miami on vacation from Maine overheard our haggling. He went over to where the Indians stood with the pony drags and began talking to them and examining their goods. The man began sorting through the crafts and making separate piles of the items that he liked. Hairpins made of turtle shell, bone smoking pipes, jewelry, leather accessories, rugged buckskin pants, and the colorful, soft, doeskin dresses were all sorted out. Soon the pony drags were empty. He loved everything!

The man asked Jumping Jack, "How much for the whole lot? How much for everything?"

My friends pointed to me, and I excused myself from the conversation with the cheapskate Slick Willie and went over to the friendly stranger. He introduced himself as Mr. L. Lucky Bean, the C.E.O. of a large mail-order company located in Maine. I explained to him that we could not take money, so he agreed to give us a bill of credit to use to order goods from his extensive mail order catalogue. He promised to locally purchase and deliver to the *Watermelon* any items that we needed that he did not personally sell from his catalogue.

The affable man offered $1,800 credit, nearly five times what the cheap son-of-a-gun Slick Willie had offered! Then he handed us a Mr. L. Lucky Bean mail-order catalogue. Running Deer went wild when he saw the compound bows and the metal arrows. Jumping Jack and Full Moon had the same excited reaction when they saw the fishing gear. I arranged to have an assortment of Burpee seeds, one sack of flour, and one sack of coffee beans, as well as a crate of live chickens and four breeding goats delivered to the *Watermelon*. Mr. Lucky Bean had no way to contact us, so he gave me his personal beeper number and asked if we might wish to contract to supply more of our fine Native American crafts on a regular basis. Lucky Bean wanted to sell our goods worldwide through his catalogue! I agreed. I felt like we had just won the lottery! We all shook hands and then my friends and I left the trading post.

"Let's celebrate!" I said.

We walked outside and went under the overpass in front of Slick Willie's Trading Post. Three homeless guys were sitting on empty paint pails and drinking bottled beer. One guy tossed a paint pail toward me. "Have a seat," he said.

The can landed at my feet and splashed yellow paint onto what was left of my black rubber dive fins.

"Oh great—as if these torn rubber shoes didn't look stupid enough! Now I've got yellow polka dots all over them!" I said.

My friends laughed loudly and pointed at my feet. The homeless guy felt bad and offered me a gift. "Sorry 'bout that, buddy. Take anything you want from our pile of junk."

The street people had been "alley shopping" and had a collection of discarded items piled under the overpass. I did not see any shoes, so I declined his offer. The guy felt bad and frowned. I tried to console him. "It's not a problem, mister. These things on my feet were my dive fins before a croc chewed them up. They're going in the trash as soon as I find a decent pair of shoes."

To show that we had no hard feelings, we gave the homeless guys our pony drags. We had no further use for them, and we figured that the street people could use them to haul their junk. The trio thought the pony drags were sheer genius. They were so grateful that the guy with the chronic, hacking cough offered us a sip of his beer. We thanked him but declined and began walking east on the Venetian Causeway toward Miami Beach.

The guy with the cough called out to us as we departed. "Hey, my friend, those rubber shoes look much better with the yellow dots! They look trendy!"

Another guy raised his beer bottle, offering a toast by yelling out, "He's right! Now those rubber shoes look beautiful, mate!"

That proved to me that

Beauty is in the eye of the beer holder!

Chapter 10

SOUTH BEACH

We began walking east on the MacArthur Causeway toward South Beach, Miami. People in passing cars honked horns and waved to us. My strange-looking band of brothers drew a lot of attention. The woman reporter and the newspaper photographer continued documenting our activities as they followed us.

The reporter's name was Rosalina. She asked if she could write a story about us for her newspaper, the Miami *Herald*. We agreed on the condition that we received a free copy of her report.

On Alton Road, a long, black stretch limo pulled over to the side of the road and stopped ahead of us. As we approached, a man sitting in the back seat rolled down the rear window and spoke with an Italian accent. "Good morning, gentlemen. My name is Giuseppe Versace, and I'm very interested in your Native American costumes. Might you find the time to accompany me to my studio so that I may examine those extraordinary outfits?"

"Hey, hey, fellows! Want to ride in a stretch limo?" I asked my friends.

"My studio is a mere four blocks away and located in my home. Of course I will compensate you for your time."

Eager to escape the afternoon heat, we happily accepted Versace's offer. We all piled into the air-conditioned stretch limo, and Rosalina leaned over and whispered in my ear, "Mr. Giuseppe Versace is a famous international fashion designer."

Versace reached out and began combing Full Moon's hair with his fingers and asked, "This is a very interesting cut. Who is your stylist?"

Full Moon did not understand the question, so I explained to Mr. Versace that a Whatchacallit warrior named Swimming Mullet had been the first person to cut his hair that way. I told him that Swimming Mullet had been inspired by the look of my hair after a huge croc tore clumps of my long hair from the crown and sides of my head.

For the first time, Versace examined my hair closely and was horrified. "This will not do! Oh, no! No! Your hair is asymmetrical, which is OK, but the quality of the cut is just awful! Oh my! That is a horrible cut! Driver, forget about my studio. This is an emergency! Take us to my friend Vidal Pontoon's salon, pronto!"

My ragged "croc cut" did not please Versace

The driver began speeding up Collins Avenue and came to a screeching halt on Collins Avenue. If I had been bleeding to death, I do not think Versace could have gotten me to an emergency room any faster than he got me to Pontoon's Hair Salon.

Versace flung the limo door open and pulled me out as he stared at my head in horror. He took the ascot from his neck and covered my hideous head as he rushed me inside. "Oh, you poor dear! Don't worry! Vidal will fix you up straight away."

The salon was a beehive of activity and became even more chaotic with the arrival of the frantic Versace and his oddball entourage.

"Vidal is not here at the moment, Mr. Versace."

"Oh my God, no! Look at this poor man. For God's sake, this is an emergency!" Versace began pacing and clapping his hands.

"Put in an emergency call to Vidal! For God's sake! Who is the best stylist available right now?"

A man stepped forward. "I'm in charge. I'm second to Vidal."

Versace grabbed Full Moon and dragged him violently by the arm over to the stylist's chair. He began running his fingers through Full Moon's layered haircut. "We need to duplicate this professional cut!" he ordered.

Versace pushed me into the chair. The stylist and a group of cosmetology students gathered around Full Moon and examined his hair. Then they surrounded me as everyone examined and compared our haircuts.

The stylist mussed up Full Moon's hair and said, "I have never seen this cut before, but it should be no problem to duplicate."

"I believe the Indians called it the Swimming Mullet cut! They told me an Indian warrior named Swimming Mullet designed the style based on Eddie Ocean's horrible haircut!" Versace was still very animated and speaking loudly as the stylist began trimming my hair.

Vidal Pontoon arrived shortly after my haircut was completed, and Versace greeted him. "Vidal, my friend, finally you have arrived! We could not wait for you! No, not even one minute! We had a dire hair emergency—quite a disaster, actually! But look now, look at how beautiful this young man's hair is now!"

Again Versace combed my hair with his fingers, but this time he was pleased. Then Vidal Pontoon began closely examining my haircut with a small, fine-toothed comb.

"Very interesting. I like this style," Vidal said.

"As I told your stylist, the Indians call it the swimming mullet," said Versace.

"I want to put this in the Pontoon catalogue. It is a perfect male style to complement my new wedged bob female style!" said Pontoon.

They paraded me around, admiring my hair and taking pictures for the catalogue.

"Did you notice those shoes, Vidal? Aren't they just marvelous! I could not focus on the shoes until that horrible hair was fixed, but I just love them!" Now Versace was focused on my chewed-off dive fins.

"Hmmm…look at those interesting shoes," Pontoon concurred.

"Where did you buy those shoes, Eddie?" Versace asked. "It looks like you might have made them yourself."

"These were once my snorkel diving fins. The same croc that bit off my hair chewed the flipper part off my fins and put all these holes in them. Then some homeless guys downtown accidentally splattered yellow paint on them." I lifted my right foot up toward Versace as I explained.

"I love them! Black with yellow polka dots—genius! I will design a whole line of those Kroc shoes…those rubber shoes with ventilation holes! I will offer a wide variety of colors and designs. Don't worry—you will get your royalties, Mr. Ocean," said Versace.

Not to be outdone by his good friend, Vidal Pontoon added, "If the swimming mullet hairstyle is a success, I will also pay your tribe and Mr. Mullet royalties."

A year later, I started seeing many people with mullet haircuts. The style was very popular in the 1980s and with many celebrities. The Kroc shoes did not catch on with the pop culture until many years later but eventually became the number-one selling style of footwear.

"Tonight I'm having a party for some celebrities from the music industry. We are honoring a new rising star named Kylie Simon. Eddie, I would like you and your friends to be my guests of honor. I want to show off the trendy, new styles that you handsome young men have brought to Miami. Tonight, after you finish your personal business, please come to this address on Star Island at 10:00 pm." Giuseppe Versace handed me a business card with the name Kylie Simon and an address scribbled on the back.

We happily accepted the invitation, and just as fast as he had arrived, Versace left with a flurry of arm waving and shouting.

The first order of business I needed to address was to visit the postmaster to get the Whatchacallit tribe added to the monthly Ten Thousand Island mail boat delivery route. The tribe would not only be conducting mail-order trade with Mr. L. Lucky Bean but also might receive royalty checks for their fashion designs. To fulfill my obligation to the ancients, it was time to put the lost tribe of Invisible Whatchacallit People on the map.

While submitting the postal delivery request, I noticed some FBI Most Wanted posters hanging on the wall. The FBI's #1 most wanted fugitive was the pirate whom we had marooned on Crocodile Island. In the FBI picture he did not have a beard, but it was clearly the same guy! The poster identified him as Dick Kimble, a doctor from Chicago who was wanted for the murder of his wife. Now I understood why the pirate had chosen to stay on the island and not return with us to Miami: He was the number-one fugitive in America.

With the help of my friends, I began making the rounds of the pubs and bars along South Beach, taking delivery orders for Bahamian Kalik Ale. Once finished, we left South Beach and walked back to the downtown Miami area. It was 8:00 pm when we went into the back service entrance of Uncle Charlie's to take my Kalik order.

Uncle Charlie's was a gay nightclub; I wondered how my Indian friends would react to a crowd of gays, so I asked Timmy, the bouncer, if we could go out front to the bar for a moment. Because it was the Friday night before Halloween, many people wore costumes, and a large crowd had arrived at the club.

The DJ announced the start of two contests. "First prize will be $100 for best costume and $100 for best stage act!" said the DJ.

My Indian friends were staring at the crowd of men; some stood with arms around each other. Then they noticed the dance floor packed with men wildly dancing with other men. I waited for their reaction.

"The Wasichu warriors are celebrating tribal brotherhood. This much like our Whatchallit warrior celebration of brotherhood," said Jumping Jack.

It was true! I realized that the scene did not seem unusual to my Indian friends because men dancing with men and women dancing among themselves were common practice during tribal rituals.

A judge with a note pad came over to us and began examining the Indian's attire—the beads, bracelets, and especially the buckskin loincloths.

"Very authentic looking," commented the judge. "Will you gentlemen also be entering the talent show?"

"We have no talents," said Running Deer.

"Yes, they will be entering! We need the money!" I interjected.

"What will we do at a Wasichu's brotherhood tribal celebration?" asked Full Moon.

"Do your disco fighting dance," I suggested.

"No, that is not appropriate for the celebration of brotherhood. Maybe we can do the Whatchacallit song of honor dance!" said Jumping Jack.

"Well, I guess that will be better than nothing," I grumbled.

The song of honor ritual was rather boring in my opinion. I doubted that the performance of that ritual song would win us first prize.

"Do we have a contestant?" The DJ asked as he played a song by Exile called "I Want to Kiss You All Over." The song had a rather slow beat.

"That is good song for song of honor dance," said Jumping Jack.

My three Indian friends charged through the crowd, bypassed the steps, and leaped high into the air and onto the stage. People applauded and cheered their flamboyant entrance. The three took positions in a straight line facing the crowd.

The Indians chanted the words of the honor song as they performed the four basic movements of the ritual.

Movement #1 gives thanks to the heavenly bodies of the night sky.

The men stand with feet together, arms held overhead and spread wide, with the palms facing toward the heavens. The head is slowly tilted back in time to the beat.

Movement #2 gives thanks to Mother Earth.

The men stand with feet together, arms spread wide below the waists, and palms facing down toward the earth, slowly tilting their heads forward and down in time with the beat.

Movement #3 gives thanks for the rising sun.

The men now spread their feet wide apart and, in time to the beat, begin leaning far to the left with fingers extended and arms forming a semi-circle.

Movement #4 gives thanks to the Great Teepee that houses the ancients in the Meadow of Tranquility.

The men make the symbol of the teepee by standing with legs wide apart, arms overhead, and hands slowly brought together until the palms touch, fingers pointing skyward, symbolizing a teepee.

The song ended, and a man in the crowd asked, "What were the Indians saying? Was that a foreign language they spoke?"

The DJ began playing a faster song.

Now my friends were making the same ritual movements at a much faster pace. It looked comical to me.

Another man called out from the crowd. "They are trying to spell something. Look—that was the letter Y!"

The Indians stood with arms spread and raised to the heavens.

"Now an M, and that must be a C! Now they're making an A!" my Indian friends stood like three teepees in a row.

"They are spelling Y.M.C.A.!" someone called out.

The crowd began calling out the letters for each of the four positions. Then many people in the crowd began making the four ritual movements while singing out the letters. "YMCA! YMCA!" People were singing, laughing, and applauding.

The DJ grabbed his mike and said; "This YMCA dance is fun!"

Someone in the crowd added a lyric: "It's fun to do the YMCA! It's fun to do the YMCA…A!"

The crowd was going wild as they roared their approval. Suddenly a biker dude dressed in black leather ran up the steps and joined my friends on stage. A man in a policeman's costume accompanied by a sailor followed him. Then a cowboy with his construction worker friend joined the dancers.

Running Deer, Biker Dude, Full Moon and
Jumping Jack perform the song of honor

"What a motley crew we have on stage! This looks like Uncle Charlie's in New York City. This could be the West Village on any given weeknight. They look like West Village dudes," said the DJ.

"Does anyone want to follow that act? No…I didn't think so! We have our talent show champions—the three little Indian boys!"

The crowd went crazy as my friends accepted a check for $100.

Two years later I did a double-take while walking past a TV in a pub. The guys from Uncle Charlie's who had joined the Whatchacallit song of honor dance ritual had formed a touring group. The group called themselves the Village Dudes. On TV, they performed the song of honor with the new Wasichu YMCA lyrics instead of the Whatchacallit Song of Honor chant. The Village Dudes recorded many hit records. The group became so popular that as of today they have sold over 100 million records worldwide.

It was after ten o'clock when Timmy, the bouncer, told us that a limo was in front of Uncle Charlie's, waiting for us. Some early arriving guests at Kylie Simon's party had told Giuseppe Versace that his three Indian friends had been seen performing on stage at Uncle Charlie's Club and probably would not be attending the party. When Giuseppe heard that news, he had a hissy fit. He ordered his driver and bodyguard to bring us back to Star Island, dead or alive. Given no choice by the burly bodyguard, who stood with one hand reaching for something hidden under his jacket, we left Uncle Charlie's and got into the limo.

The limo pulled up to a Star Island home, and we were informed that this was where Kylie Simon was staying. I did not know of her, but I was told that she was a young singer who had just won the award for best new vocalist. We were escorted to a beautifully landscaped backyard with wide water views of Biscayne Bay. Many celebrities mingled there under the trees, some of whom had arrived by yachts anchored behind the residence.

My Indian friends immediately attracted everyone's attention. People gathered around us asking questions about our tribe; then we were introduced to Kylie Simon. She was a very nice girl.

Suddenly the crowd lost interest in Kylie when a fellow dressed all in white arrived. He wore a white linen suit adorned with a long, apricot-colored scarf and had a white fedora hat tipped down low on his brow. He was smoking a cigarette from a long, elegant cigarette holder as he made his grand entrance. The crowd flocked around the man, but he pretty much ignored them; he was too busy admiring himself in a full-length mirror.

We were left standing alone in the yard with Kylie Simon, and she seemed perturbed. She said, "He's a pain! He walked into my party like he was walking onto his yacht. He probably thinks this party is about him. He's a pain!"

"Who is that fancy fellow?" asked Jumping Jack.

"That's the famous Nick Dagger, Mr. Tumbling Stone himself. He had me many years ago when I was still quite naïve. Now he's just clouds in my coffee," Kylie said poetically.

I realized that Kylie and this Dagger fellow must have once been a couple but were now not so friendly. The pair must have made up later that night, though because, about a year after I met them, Nick Dagger and Kylie Simon recorded a song together. It was called *"You're a Pain"* and was obviously written by Kylie about Nick's rude entrance to her party.

The crowd around him gradually thinned, and we introduced ourselves to Mr. Dagger. He was actually very friendly and seemed to be a very nice fellow. I noticed that he was constantly dabbing a tooth with clove oil. Nick told us that he was suffering from a toothache.

"Fellow, me know a much better medicine for toothache than clove oil," said Jumping Jack as he pointed into the branches of a large banyan tree. Long strands of gray moss hung from its branches.

Nick, who was sitting beneath the tree in an Adirondack-style chair sipping a cocktail, said to Jumping Jack, "Mate, if you can get rid of my toothache I would be so grateful. I would write a song about you!"

"That moss up there...strong tooth medicine! I be right back!" Jumping Jack scampered up the tree and high into the branches with little effort. The crowd of celebrities applauded his agility, speed, and strength.

"That Indian went up that tree in a flash!" someone commented.

Jumping Jack noticed that he was now the center of attention. Due to all the attention that he had been receiving from the Wasichu people lately, Jumping Jack was becoming quite a ham. He began making monkey sounds while swinging through the branches. People laughed at his antics. Then he began jumping from branch to branch, which made the crowd gasp, fearing for his safety.

"That Jumping Jack is a gas!" said Dagger as he laughed loudly.

Still acting like a monkey, Jumping Jack tossed wads of moss to the ground below, and my friends and I began to gather them up. We noticed that Dagger did not offer to help us even though the moss was for his benefit.

With lightning speed, Jumping Jack came back down to the ground and rolled a clump of moss into a compacted wad. He showed Nick how to put the pinch between his cheek and gum. After twenty minutes, Nick was ecstatic—his toothache was gone.

"Not only is the pain gone, but I feel euphoric! Thank you, Jumping Jack!"

He turned to Kylie and asked her: "Kylie, sweetheart, will you collect the rest of that moss and put it into a bag for me, sweet dear?" Nick crooned in a syrupy voice.

"Do it yourself, you lazy Limey son of a gun!" She was still angry.

We collected the moss for Nick, and as we left the party to return to the *Watermelon*, Running Deer commented, "Nick Dagger is a very nice fellow, but he sure likes to be pampered."

"He's the lead singer for the Tumbling Stones band. He's very famous and, like many celebrities, he expects to be waited on," I replied.

"He should have at least picked up his own moss," said Jumping Jack.

That brought to mind a truism:

A Tumbling Stone gathers no moss!

Chapter 11

FAREWELL FEAST AT VERSAILLES

At 2:30 am we left Kylie Simon's party and returned to the *Watermelon* to spread our bedrolls above deck. The traffic noise and bright lights from the vibrant city thwarted our attempted to get some much-needed sleep. With great difficulty due to the light pollution from downtown Miami, I identified Orion's belt, my trusty friend of the night sky. The three stars of his belt were all that were visible, but they reminded me of the night I had spent with Little Hooters at the Kissing Place.

Is she awake and thinking of me or sleeping soundly in her parents' lodge? I wondered.

Exhaustion finally overcame my restlessness, and I fell into a deep sleep until another vision concerning Little Hooters came to me.

In this vision, Little Hooters had married Jumping Jack. I saw them playing games with their young son and a daughter. Little Hooters appeared to be very happy, as were her parents and Jumping Jack's relatives. Then I saw myself, sad and alone, sailing solo toward the setting sun. In the distance, the desolate and foreboding shore of a strange land awaited me.

Once again it was difficult to know if I was having a bad dream or being given a vision by the ancients. I was confused until an ancient spirit spoke to me in the vision:

"Sun Chaser Eddie Ocean, you are not dreaming. We have given you this vision into your future. It is not your destiny to take a wife at this time in your life. The woman you love is not part of your destiny. She is meant for another man. You have much work to do before you settle down and have a family. You have many dangerous places to travel. It would not be fair for you to leave a wife alone for years at a time, not fair to endanger her life by taking her with you, not fair to separate her from her family and her people."

I awoke in a sweat with my heart pounding. I felt that familiar sickness of longing and heartbreak. The vision saddened me, and I did not want to believe it was a true vision.

I was in denial: *It must have just been a bad dream, a nightmare.*

I did not want to accept the future that had been revealed to me. *Yes, it was! The vision was false, just a nightmare, a bad dream, and a creation of my own mind.*

I fell back into a fitful, dreamless sleep.

It was 7:00 am when the sound of a horn woke us. Giuseppe Versace's limo was on the pier next to the *Watermelon*. His driver got out and informed us that we were all invited to breakfast. Versace was in the back seat with Nick Dagger and Kylie Simon.

"Come, my friends—join us for breakfast!" Versace called out from the back seat's window.

We were famished and happily piled into the limo, and I was glad for the diversion. I could not stop thinking about my horrible nightmare; fear of losing Little Hooters overwhelmed me.

It was apparent that Nick, Giuseppe, and Kylie had not slept. They said that they had been up all night songwriting.

Nick wore a black wig and eyeglasses with thick black frames. He looked very nerdy.

"Is that your Halloween costume?" I asked him.

"No, just a disguise to keep a bit of privacy, mate. I hate those paparazzi, you know."

The driver took us to the Little Havana section of Miami and pulled over at a restaurant located on SW 8th Street. A sign identified the place as Versailles Cuban Restaurant. The scant attire of my Indian friends was not an issue; many diners had come from all-night Halloween parties, and some wore outrageous costumes.

Giuseppe ordered for our entire party. He ordered half the items on the extensive breakfast menu. The large order kept a line of waiters busy delivering platters to our table. My Indian friends scarfed down the strange but delicious delicacies. I ate a Basque Omelet, Mariquitas with Mojo, and FuFu Con Masitas, and washed it all down with guava and mango juice. After my belly was full I enjoyed a Cortadito, a coffee drink. The Indians ate even more than I. In the Whatchacallit culture it is impolite to turn away food offerings, so they gleefully ate themselves to the bursting point.

"You blokes would clean out the entire food supply of the U.K. in less than a week!" said Dagger as he daintily nibbled a fruit salad.

To express his gratitude for the wonderful feast, Jumping Jack leaned sideways in his seat and emitted a resounding fart, followed by an explosive belch. Dagger laughed loudly at my friend's lack of inhibition. I explained to my Wasichu friends that flatulence was meant as a compliment to the host and the cooks.

"That Jumping Jack is a gas!" said Dagger as he tried unsuccessfully to belch.

Full Moon and Running Deer reciprocated successfully and loudly. Dagger finally managed a meager fart as Giuseppe Versace and Kylie Simon sat silently in horror and embarrassment at our group's lack of etiquette. Diners in the area looked at us in disgust. Dagger noticed the hostile faces and responded by gulping in air and then successfully burping loudly.

"Nick! Why do you have to act so immature! You will never grow up!" whined Kylie.

Versace took Kylie's scarf from her and used it to hide his face as he called for the check. Dagger grabbed the check from the waiter's hand and paid with a wad of cash as Giuseppe and Kylie literally ran from the restaurant. Dagger and my three Indian friends weren't done complimenting the restaurant workers for the fine meal that had been provided, however. They walked to the service area and paid the chef and the servers more gaseous salutations.

Once in the limo Dagger could not control his laughter as Kylie berated him for his inappropriate behavior and pounded her fist into his shoulder. Giuseppe continued to cover his head and just wanted to get away, as he ordered the limo driver to take us to the Vizcaya Museum. Giuseppe was very knowledgeable on the subject of the fine arts, and he gave us a guided tour of the Vizcaya palace and gardens. We spent the rest of the afternoon seeing many sights in Miami; again I appreciated the diversion. My entertaining and generous friends provided me relief from the nightmarish vision that continued to haunt me.

By 3:00 pm our energetic host, Versace, had finally grown tired. He returned us to the *Watermelon* but before leaving invited us to yet another party. This one was planned for later that night at his mansion.

"Don't you people ever sleep?" I asked.

We accepted the invitation but told Versace we could not stay overnight because we were sailing out of Miami on Sunday morning. Our new celebrity friends were disappointed to learn of our pending departure.

"If you must leave us, then the party tonight will be in honor of you, my new friends. We will give you a grand bon voyage party tonight! I will send my limo for you at 10:00 o'clock sharp," said Giuseppe.

We climbed out of the limo at the pier. A delivery truck was waiting for us beside my boat. After signing the manifest, we helped two men unload the goods that had been ordered from Mr. Lucky Bean's catalogue. Along with the dry goods and camping/sporting equipment, there was a crate containing four live chickens and one bossy little bantam rooster. The last item offloaded was a large cage containing four goats. Everything was transferred onto the *Watermelon*. We put dog collars on the goats and led them out of the pen with rope leashes and tied them to cleats at the bow of the boat. Now they could move about without running off into the city.

By the time all the cargo was stowed away, it was already 5:00 pm. A shaded area on deck provided relief from the sun as we popped open some Kalik ale to rehydrate our tired bodies; then we napped.

At 10:00 pm Versace's limo arrived and drove us to his mansion. The bon voyage party was already underway, and a band was playing disco music. The exuberant, well-hydrated crowd begged the Indians to perform the Y.M.C.A. song of honor dance that some had witnessed at Uncle Charlie's.

"This music not good for Song of Honor dance. This music better for disco fighting dance," said Jumping Jack.

The Indians associated disco music and disco dancing movements with a war dance, a dance of violence, not with the song of honor dance that symbolized peace and brotherhood. The crowd's disappointment at not seeing the YMCA dance quickly vanished. My three friends pulled me out onto the dance floor, and the four of us began disco dancing. We added wild, high leaps and powerful throws to the traditional disco moves.

"Hoka hey!" we yelled as we tossed one another about to the beat of the music.

The crowd cheered and applauded when the song came to an end. "More! More! More!" the crowd clapped and chanted.

I escaped to the sidelines and mingled with the crowd to hide from my friends. The three Indians stood in a line on the dance floor. Jumping Jack must have recalled the time that Dancing Bird and I performed the chicken dance for the tribe. He announced, "Now we will perform the white man's war dance! The dance that

Sun Chaser Eddie Ocean taught to the Whatchacallit people! The Wasichu warriors chicken dance," said Jumping Jack.

The three Indians had a brief discussion. Then the band began playing another song.

Jumping Jack put his hands behind his back and began strutting around like a rooster to the disco beat. The other two formed their hands into the shape of beaks and began pecking at Jumping Jack. To avoid the attack, Jumping Jack began spinning and hopping high in the air like a fighting cock as the other two strutted and chased him back and forth. Nick Dagger thought they were hilarious. He laughed uncontrollably as he put his hands on his hips and strutted out onto the dance floor.

Then, like a spastic rooster, Nick strutted over to the microphone and began singing the lyrics to the new song that he had written the night of Kylie Simon's party. The song was written to thank Jumping Jack for giving Nick the toothache remedy. Nick called the song

"Jack Flash."

Nick strutted back and forth, hands on hips, legs flailing wildly like a rooster, as the Indians danced and strutted wildly behind him.

"Jumping Jack is a gas." Dagger sang.

"Nick singing 'bout me! That my song! Song Nick promised for me!" said Jumping Jack as he began chicken-strutting in a circle around Nick.

"Jumping Jack" became a major hit for the Tumbling Stones band, and to this day, when Nick performs at concerts, he often uses the "chicken strut" that he learned from my Indian friends.

Our bon voyage party was a great success. After the party, Versace's limo returned us to the *Watermelon*. It was just after 2:00 am, and we found a collie dog sitting in the boat, barking at our goats. The dog had the goats cornered up in the bow section of the boat. I was about to chase the dog away when the dockmaster drove up in a golf cart.

"You people are lucky you have that dog. Your goats chewed through their ropes, got loose, and were wandering into the traffic on Biscayne Boulevard! Nobody could catch them until your collie dog herded them back onto the boat for you. He's kept them there all night."

"He's not our dog. Never saw him before," I said.

"Well, you should give him a reward. Your goats were almost road kill tonight."

Running Deer knelt in front of the dog and spoke softly in Whatchacallit as he petted him. The dog whimpered and panted heavily.

"Dog says…want water."

Full Moon went below deck and got a bowl of fresh water for the dog.

I looked at the tag on his collar. "There's no name. Just a registration number. I wonder what his name is?"

"Dog," said Running Deer.

"Yes, the dog. What's the dog's name?" I said.

"Dog." Running Deer repeated. I thought Running Deer had gone daft.

Jumping Jack attempted to clarify the confusion. "The dog is saying that his name is Dog."

"So you fellows can talk to this dog?"

My Indian friends looked at me like I had two heads. "Of course! Dog communicate much better than you…much better than most Wasichu people," said Jumping Jack.

We re-tied the goats, fed all the animals including Dog, and fell into a deep sleep. Dog slept near the goats, guarding them.

SUNDAY, OCTOBER 28TH, 1973

Again a honking horn woke us. This time it was 7:00 am Sunday. Rosalina stood on the pier beside her car. She reached in through the open window and honked the horn twice more to arouse us.

"Wake up, you sleepyheads. You guys are local celebrities! You will soon be the talk of Miami."

She held four copies of the Sunday edition of the Miami *Herald* under her arm. Walking to our boat, she removed a section from the middle of each of the thick newspapers. We all took a copy of the "Entertainment Today" section. Rosalina had written a cover story about our recent escapades in Miami. The lengthy article included several color photographs.

"We good-looking fellows!" commented Jumping Jack.

We were getting ready to depart and asked Rosalina if she could take Dog and find his master. She agreed to help, but when we tried to put Dog in her car, he ran away toward the city.

"Well, I guess he'll find his own way home," she said.

We said our farewells, and Rosalina drove off.

The *Watermelon* had been fueled, and we were ready to cast off. The outgoing tide was running strong when we tossed off the dock lines at 8:00 am. Jumping Jack pushed the bow away from the pier and then jumped aboard. Out of the corner of my eye, I saw a flash of tan and white streaking toward the boat. The streak followed Jumping Jack, leaping onto the *Watermelon* just at the last instant. It was Dog!

"Hey! What do you think you're doing?" I yelled at the dog. He looked at me mischievously, with a toothy grin.

"That smart dog...he want come with us," said Running Deer as he began rubbing the animal's head. Then he added, "Dog says he want job. He want to herd goats for us."

"What about his owner? We can't steal the dog," I said.

The dog made a series of barks and whimpering sounds.

"Dog say that his master is cruel. Cruel man kick Dog and beat boy with belt! Boy is cruel man's son. Master beat boy, so Dog bite master's hand. Dog cannot go home now...bad man will kill Dog! Dog want job with us instead," said Running Deer.

"I can't believe you are telling me this load of crap! You made up that story because you want to keep the dog...right?" I asked.

"I just say what Dog tell me," said Running Deer.

"Running Deer speaks true...that what Dog say," added Full Moon.

"Well, some day you fellows might teach me how to talk to animals. If we are going to keep this dog we should give him a proper name. Ask Dog what we should call him," I said.

"Cruel master hate dog, but boy love Dog. Cruel master not let boy name dog," said Running Deer.

Jumping Jack had an idea. "We found Dog on *Watermelon* boat. We should call him Watermelon Boat Dog," said Jumping Jack.

"OK, but that's a mouth full. How about Melon Dog for short? That's easier," I said.

The collie began barking excitedly and leaping up to lick Running Deer's face. "Dog say he like new name."

"Melon Dog very happy!" said Running Deer.

"Even I can see that!" I said.

We sailed out of Government Cut and into the Atlantic Ocean. The handsome young collie stood at the bow, sniffing the scent of the ocean and scouting the sea ahead of us as the stiff breeze ruffled his thick fur coat. He probably had never been in a boat before, but he seemed to be enjoying the experience. The restless goats had never been to sea either and began to climb up onto the cuddy cabin roof until the collie barked a command at them. The goats immediately came back down from the roof and behaved themselves. The proud collie seemed to be gloating over his newfound authority as he stood facing the goats with a toothy grin.

Gazing at the horizon, I steered the boat, and my heart sank. The horrible vision haunted me, and I realized that we would be home in four days' time. *What should I say to Little Hooters? Should I reveal my vision of her being married to Jumping Jack?*

I did not want to tell her about us not having a future together in the vision.

No, it was not a vision! It was only a nightmare! A bad dream that was so vivid that it only felt like a vision.

My mind was racing.

Do I really not have a future with Little Hooters? I wondered as I watched Jumping Jack trimming the mainsail. The vision of him and Little Hooters happily married with children at their side and me alone on the sea would not leave my mind. My sadness deepened, but then I recalled what Little Hooters had said to me at the Kissing Place.

"Our destinies will find us," she had said.

If the nightmare was truly a vision, then the life revealed to me by the ancients was not the fate I had hoped for.

The collie must have sensed my sadness. He walked over to me, rubbed against my leg, and licked my ankle to comfort me. I rubbed his head. "You are a good boy, Melon Dog."

Ever since kissing Little Hooters, I had been walking on clouds. The past week of my life had been the happiest time I've ever known. Then I had that horrible vision into the future. Now the collie's empathy for my sudden sadness made me realize that just when everything seems to be going your way,

Sometimes life will leave you a little melon collie!

Chapter 12

THE BLACK SAIL

TUESDAY, OCTOBER 30TH, 1973

On the third day at sea, Crocodile Island was visible in the distance. We adjusted our course so that the boat would skirt the southern beach, the area where we had marooned the pirate Dick Kimble. I wondered if he had survived. The *Watermelon* entered the shallows just off the beach, and I asked Full Moon to keep a lookout on the water and the surf. I feared that the dreaded croc a bull gator might be lying in wait for prey on the bottom.

No sign of Kimble could be seen on the island, so to the relief of my companions I set a course for home and began sailing out to sea. I had traveled only a short distance when we heard a commotion. Kimble came running from the jungle and onto the beach, calling for us to come back. I jibbed, bringing the boat about, and returned to the shallow water just off the beach. From waist-deep water, Jumping Jack pulled Kimble up and into the boat.

Moments later we heard something crashing through the underbrush in the jungle. The mutant croc burst from beneath the tree line, charging full speed across the beach toward us. I noticed that his huge jaws were discolored, burned, and charred black. The miserable beast was still alive and in an even fouler mood than usual.

"Whatchacallit! Get us out of here, Sun Chaser!" screamed Full Moon.

A gust of wind filled the sail and began propelling us into deep water, but the croc was not eager to let us depart. He hoped to have us stay for dinner. With swift, short, choppy steps, he crossed the beach to the water's edge and then dove into the surf. Gliding effortlessly through the water just below the surface, he approached us with surprising speed. Like a giant green torpedo, the croc took aim at the stern of the *Watermelon* and rammed us hard. The boat shuddered, and water splashed up and over the transom as the croc lifted his massive head into the boat and began trying to climb aboard. Melon Dog ran toward the croc barking as my crew and I ran away toward the bow of the boat to regroup and escape the snapping jaws. The cowardly pirate dove headfirst below deck and hid there under a blanket as the frightened goats took refuge above him by climbing atop the cuddy cabin.

The monster got its front legs onto the transom and began climbing. His enormous weight made the bow rise up out of the water as the stern was pushed downward. I feared that the transom might be forced below the water line, which would swamp the boat. Melon Dog growled and barked as he nimbly evaded the snapping jaws by darting back and forth in front of the croc's face. The little dog was fearless and ferocious in his attempt to defend us.

Suddenly, the bow jerked upward even higher as the croc got both of its front legs into the boat and onto the deck. At the bow, we all held onto the standing rigging to avoid sliding down the deck toward the stern and into the croc's jaws. The boat began rocking up and down, and the boom was swinging uncontrollably from side to side as the *Watermelon* floundered in the stiff breeze.

Suddenly, the boom swung hard to port just three feet above the cuddy cabin roof. The goats ducked low to avoid being struck, but one was knocked from the cuddy cabin roof by the heavy boom of the sail. The helpless animal fell, landing on its back, and slid down the inclined deck toward the stern. Right into the croc's jaws he went!

The croc snapped his jaws shut, crushing the goat with a crunching sound, and flipped his head up to reposition the goat's carcass in its mouth. As he began swallowing the goat whole, he pushed off from the stern and disappeared below the surface of the ocean directly behind our boat. Melon Dog stood atop the transom, barking furiously at the empty, open ocean. At the helm, I regained control of the boat and sailed away as fast as the stiff breeze would carry us. I feared that at any moment the beast would come back for dessert.

"Goat sacrificed self. Goat save Melon Dog…goat now with the animal spirits!" said Running Deer.

"The goat got knocked into the croc's jaws by the boom of our sail," I said.

"Goat not scared…goat not make a sound! Goat not call for us to help! Goat die to save Melon Dog," insisted Running Deer.

"Running Deer speaks truth. The dog has strong spirit… powerful medicine. Goat might have died to save his guardian dog," said Jumping Jack.

"Melon Dog very brave! He warrior dog," agreed Full Moon.

I had great love and respect for my friends but did not understand their strange beliefs or relate to their mysticism. I had gained much wisdom from them concerning man's relationship with nature and had learned many wondrous things from the Whatchacallit people, but I doubted that they were actually able to communicate with animals, especially wild ones that were not pets.

Melon Dog was loyal to all of us, but the dog had formed a special bond with the hunter, Running Deer. After the death of the goat, the dog approached Running Deer whimpering and lay submissively at his feet.

"Melon Dog say he very sorry. Sorry he not protect goat," said Running Deer as the dog whimpered. Running Deer spoke in the Whatchacallit tongue to the dog and rubbed his head.

"I tell dog we proud of him…he brave dog. Dog feel better." The dog came to each of us, and we patted his head to reassure him; then he went over to the three surviving goats and licked their faces. In mourning, the goats bayed loudly.

"Goats not blame Melon Dog," said Running Deer.

Suddenly Melon Dog began growling again.

"What is it, boy? Is the croc coming back?" I asked.

Kimble emerged from the cuddy cabin, and the dog growled at the stinky pirate.

"Did you kill that horrible beast?" Kimble asked.

"We should have fed *you* to the croc, you criminal, you coward! I saw a WANTED poster of you at the post office in Miami!" I said.

The pirate responded, "I didn't want to tell you until now—I'm not really a pirate. I'm a doctor—a surgeon—and I'm wanted for murder, but I'm innocent."

"I suspected that you weren't really a pirate! You can't sail a boat, you can't fight, and you're a coward! That puffy white pirate shirt looks like you bought it at a Halloween costume store," I said.

'The 1700s are calling and want their puffy pirate shirt back," Full Moon said, mocking the man.

We laughed at the joke, but Kimble was not amused.

"I'm a vascular surgeon from Chicago. My name is Dick Kimble. I can't return to the U.S. mainland because I'm accused of murdering my wife—but I'm *innocent!* A one-armed man killed my wife, not I. I joined the pirates to hide from the FBI. Most of the pirates are wanted criminals. They helped me get a fake ID and passage on The Black Sail—a vessel that will be traveling the Great Loop back to Chicago," said Kimble.

"The Great Loop? Isn't that the name for the series of waterways that lead from the Atlantic Ocean inland, all the way through the Great Lakes and as far west as Chicago?" I asked.

"Yes. As I said, I'm a surgeon, but I have a fake ID and a new identity as an orderly working in a Chicago hospital. I hope to return undercover...return to Chicago to clear my name and find the one-armed man who murdered my wife," he said.

"This all sounds like a wild fantasy that you dreamed up while you were marooned on Crocodile Island, a story devised so that we would help you," I said.

"I'm telling the truth! You saw my WANTED poster! If you'll put me off on Pine Island, I will never bother you again, Mr. Ocean. My pirate friends had booked me passage aboard the Black Sail, the ship that will return me to Chicago. In three days, she is scheduled to arrive at Pine Island and then sail the Great Loop," said Kimble.

"We will pass Pine Island in two days. But if I take you there, how do I know the Pine Island pirates won't attack us again?" I asked.

"I know the secret signal, the signal of free passage. You'll be safe."

I was skeptical but didn't know what else to do with the man, so I agreed to return him to Pine Island. Years later, I discovered that Dick Kimble's story was true. Twenty years later a movie titled *The Fugitives* was released. The story was based on Dr. Dick Kimble's experience as a fugitive from the FBI. Sadly, Kimble's adventure as a faux pirate was edited out of the movie. Despite that directorial error in judgment, *The Fugitives* was a Hollywood blockbuster. Dr. Kimble cleared his name and found his wife's murderer, the one-armed man.

We sailed for two days more before I saw the large Australian pine trees on the horizon. I called Kimble. "We are five miles off Pine Island. What is the pirates' signal of free passage?" I asked him.

"We need to raise the pirates' flag—the Jolly Roger. The black skull and crossbones flag," he said.

"What! I don't carry a pirates' flag! Are you crazy?"

"I thought all sailors had one of those flags," said Kimble.

"You're an idiot, Kimble!"

"Maybe we could paint a piece of sailcloth with the pirate symbol—that might work," said Full Moon.

"The flag must be black or they will know you are a poseur," said Kimble.

I continued sailing while my crew and Kimble searched the boat for materials from which we could fashion a pirates' flag. They came up empty. We had no black cloth or paint. I was about to change course to avoid the island when I saw a tall-rigged sailing ship approaching us from astern.

"Look astern! A tall ship with black sails is approaching!" I said

"That is the Black Sail, my ride back to Chicago! She must be a day ahead of schedule!" said Kimble.

I let the sail luff, bringing the *Watermelon* to a stop. We drifted and waited for the Black Sail to catch up to us. As the Black Sail drew near, I started the engine. When the ship came alongside, I could not believe my eyes! I wondered if Dr. Kimble had slipped me a hallucinogenic drug. Two dozen little people, miniature pirates with eye patches and headscarves, stood along the starboard rail of the Black Sail screaming down and threatening us with little wooden swords.

Upon closer examination, I realized that these were children not more than twelve years old. They cheered with delight when my crew, dressed in their Indian attire, responded by standing along our port rail challenging the young pirates and making threatening motions with their fishing spears.

"Hoka hey! You pirates are in our waters, hoka hey!" Full Moon called out.

Melon Dog began barking at the Black Sail pirates, not understanding that this fake attack was just for fun.

The pirate boys threatened us. "*Arrrgghh!* We will send you and that mangy mutt down to Davy Jones's locker, you landlubbers!"

Kimble explained to me that this was the same replica pirate boat that had brought him from Chicago down to Pine Island. It was a floating boarding school/adventure excursion that catered to the children of very wealthy Chicagoans. Kimble said there were several adults onboard the tall ship: the captain, a tutor, a cook, and a deck hand. Kimble said that he had been hired in Chicago to work as a pirate/medical officer for the southbound leg of the adventure cruise.

An adult male, also dressed like a pirate and wearing a black triangular hat, came to the rail. "Ahoy! Is that Dr. Kimble I see? Have you been taken captive by these savages, sir?"

"Ahoy, captain! Yes, it is I! These scallywags have shanghaied me. They have given me a choice. I'm to be keelhauled or forced to walk the plank!" said Kimble.

Kimble whispered to me, "This is all part of the game. Make me walk the gangplank. I'll use the bowsprit. After I go over, I will swim to the Black Sail to escape, and you will be rid of me forever".

Kimble walked to the bow with his arms raised over his head as the children howled with glee.

"Let our doctor go, you scallywag dogs!" ordered a young pirate.

Full Moon pointed his spear at the small of Kimble's back and prodded him out onto the bowsprit. Kimble pretended to be terrified and resisted walking the plank. When he reached the end of the bowsprit, he stepped into thin air and plunged down into the sea. The children screamed their approval.

Kimble swam to the Black Sail as the children lowered a rope ladder and cheered him on, and then he climbed up the side of the ship to the deck of the Black Sail. With Kimble safely onboard I gave him a farewell salute and began to motor away.

"These hostiles will pay dearly for taking our good doctor hostage! Man the cannon, boys!" the captain ordered.

The deckhand helped the children wheel an authentic-looking cast iron cannon to the gunwale. They pushed the muzzle through a firing port amidships and took aim.

"Holy whatchacallit! They are not game-playing! They are going to sink us!" cried Running Deer.

I saw the deckhand light a fuse atop the cannon; it was aiming directly at our hull. I throttled the *Watermelon* full speed forward to escape, and we all ducked for cover. The children were going wild in anticipation of the explosion.

BOOM! There was a bright flash followed by a cloud of smoke rising above the muzzle. The deafening sound hurt my ears.

"They missed! Hoka hey! They missed. The spirits protect us!" exclaimed Full Moon.

I realized that there had been no cannonball loaded. The Black Sail had fired a blank shot. My friends had no knowledge of firearms or what firing blanks meant. I did not tell them that the cannon was firing blanks, and they continued to pray and thank the spirits for protecting us. As I watched the Black Sail grow small on the horizon I set our course for home.

We were two days from homeport, and our mission was now nearly complete. We had been very fortunate considering all the adversity that we had overcome. Our only tragic loss was one of our precious goats. My great adversary and menace, the mutant croc a bull gator, had finally won a battle, this time

He really got my goat!

Chapter 13

HOMEWARD BOUND

WEDNESDAY, OCTOBER 31ST, 1973, 07:11 AM

On Halloween morning, I was sailing the *Watermelon* on a heading of 45 degrees north by northeast when the sun broke over the horizon, illuminating the eastern sky in a spectacular light show of red, pink, and blue. My crew began to stir below deck; as usual they awoke hungry. We were one day away from our homeport, and our supply of dried salt fish was gone. Jumping Jack relieved me at the helm, and I went below deck to rustle up some grub. I found two cans of black beans and opened the sack of flour. Pancakes and hot beans would be the special of the day. To me, the food pairing tasted odd, but my crew gobbled it up and then asked for seconds.

After breakfast I was about to go below deck for some shuteye when Jumping Jack said that he and the crew wanted to talk with me.

"You're not planning a mutiny, I hope." I said to my friends as we gathered at the helm.

"We want to talk to you about Little Hooters," said Jumping Jack.

That surprised me. I had promised Little Hooters I would not talk to Jumping Jack about her until we returned home.

"We know that Little Hooters asked the elders for permission to look upon you, Sun Chaser," said Jumping Jack.

I was taken off guard; I did not know that it was public knowledge. "Little Hooters asked me not to speak of that until she could tell you first. She wanted to speak to you in person, Jumping Jack."

"We not talk about Little Hooters while on mission. Warrior brothers never talk personal matters when on mission. Warrior brothers never let personal problems get in way of mission. Now mission almost over. Now we warriors must talk," said Jumping Jack.

"We all—all three of us—are looking upon Little Hooters. Eight other Whatchacallit warriors have also received permission to court Little Hooters, but Little Hooters only ask to look upon Jumping Jack and now you," said Running Deer.

"You *all* are courting Little Hooters?" I was surprised.

"It is an honor to her family that so many warriors asked to look upon their daughter, Little Hooters. She and her parents will choose her husband. It is not up to us to choose. This is the way of the Whatchacallit people," said Full Moon.

Jumping Jack added, "I hope to make Little Hooters my wife, but if she chooses you or another warrior, I will not fight her decision. Nothing must break the brotherhood bond of the Whatchacallit warriors."

Then Jumping Jack smacked me hard on the shoulder. "*Whatchacallit!*" he yelled.

The honor and honesty of the Indian people continued to impress me. I could see why Jumping Jack was such a strong leader among the men; he was honest, noble, and humble.

Then, in turn, each man slapped one another hard and called out, "Whatcahcallit!" "Whatchacallit!" "Whatchacallit!"

"Dang, that hurts!" I said, rubbing my shoulder as the three stout Indians laughed.

I considered telling them of my vision, the vision that revealed that Jumping Jack and Little Hooters were destined to be married, but I thought better of that. I was not ready to give up my dream of being with Little Hooters forever. I knew destiny would eventually take its course, but I still hoped for some say in the outcome of my fate.

Relieved to have my relationship with Little Hooters out in the open, I no longer bore the burden of that secret. After taking one more look at the spectacular sunrise I went below deck and climbing into my hammock. Sleep came quickly, and when I awoke it was 3:00 pm. I felt great! During my sleep I had dreamed of Little Hooters and me sailing together on the open sea. We were together aboard the *Watermelon*. I knew the dream was not a vision into the future, merely a dream, but I was comforted by it nevertheless.

"What is our position?" I asked Jumping Jack as I relieved him at the helm.

"We will be home by the next sunrise. Home for breakfast time—yum-yum," said Jumping Jack.

"You fellows are always thinking about food," I said.

"Eating and fishing heap good! My second and third favorite thing to do," said Jumping Jack.

THURSDAY, NOVEMBER 1ST, 1973

At 2:00 am I relieved Full Moon at the helm. This was the final leg of our voyage. I was now sailing on a heading of 90 degrees due east. We would be home shortly after dawn. The moon was just a sliver, a small crescent high in the sky, and the night was dark. At 4:00 am a large whale surfaced just off the bow, and I had no time to take evasive action. We passed just a few feet from the huge mammal, narrowly averting disaster. I could see the whale's large, round eye just a few feet away, gazing curiously at me, and then there was a loud *whoosh* as the whale blew a spout of water from his blowhole. The misty spray showered me and wet my face. I hoped the salty baptism was a sign of good luck to come.

At 6:30 am the eastern sky began to lighten the darkness, and I could see the coast of my beloved home, Florida. The hostile islands of Crocodile and Big Pine were now a distant memory. My emotions now were mixed; I longed to see Little Hooters' smiling face but did not want to tell her about my vision. At 7:11 am the sun broke over the land, and I enjoyed another gorgeous display of light and color, courtesy of Mother Nature. Again my crew awoke grumbling about being hungry. I chased hunger out of their minds when I called out, "Land ahoy!"

They scrambled up to the deck and began hollering and celebrating when they saw the coastline of Florida. "*Whatchacallit!*" They then began the painful and annoying ritual of shoulder smacking.

"Oww!" I whined as usual.

As she told me later, Little Hooters had risen with the sun. For the third sunrise in a row she walked to the Kissing Point and climbed high into the branches of an Australian pine tree. She scanned the western horizon, looking for the *Watermelon*, and then sighed with disappointment when she saw only open water. Perched on a branch high in the tree, she reclined against the trunk, looked up through the branches, and began humming an ancient Whatchacallit love song. A curious little red cardinal landed on a branch just above her head and peered down at her.

"You are a handsome little fellow with your high, red-feathered hat," she said to the bird.

She sang more of the song to the little redbird. The bird cocked his head sideways to better hear the sweet sound of her voice. When she stopped, the cardinal reciprocated by singing an intricate bird-song of rapid chirps and whistles. "Sweet...Sweet...Sweet! Pretty... Pretty...Pretty!"

"That *is* a pretty song." she said. Suddenly the cardinal flew away as a huge frigate bird landed in the tree.

"Well, who invited you to the party, Mr. Frigate? I wish I could send you out to sea to search for my friends on the *Watermelon*."

As if the bird understood her wish, he made a loud squawk and looked westward. Then he squawked again even louder, still looking westward. Little Hooters sat upright on the tree limb and looked to the horizon.

"What are you fussing about, Mr. Frigate?" She squinted her eyes and saw a small, white speck that was barely visible where the sea and the sky met on the horizon.

"It's a sail! That might be the *Watermelon*! Thank you, Mr. Frigate! I had almost given up hope! Thank you!" The large bird looked back down at Little Hooters and squawked rapidly.

"You would do that for me? Thank you!" she said.

Then the frigate bird took flight. He soared high into the air on his long, majestic wings and flew westward toward the boat. Little Hooters watched the white sail grow larger on the horizon. Then she scrambled down the tree and ran to the village to alert the people that the *Watermelon* was coming home.

We had no salted fish, and I was too excited to cook pancakes, so I asked the crew to bring up some Kalik ale.

"We will have a feast in a couple of hours when we get home. We might as well stay well hydrated in the meantime. Let's celebrate!" I said as I pulled open a pop-top.

I steered the boat, but my crew was too excited to sit back and enjoy the ride. They stood at the bow jabbering in the Whatchacallit tongue while sipping the bitterroot water and toasting the familiar landmass as we drew closer to shore.

I noticed a large frigate bird flying out to sea. I was surprised when he veered toward us and landed on our portside spreader. He began squawking, and the three Indians responded. I know not what they said because they again spoke rapidly in Whatchacallit.

"Frigate bird say bird woman sitting in tree welcomes us home," said Running Deer.

Then the bird flew west into the Gulf of Mexico to find his breakfast.

We navigated the narrow, shallow inlet that leads back to the Whatchacallit village. When we rounded the last bend, we saw a large crowd of people extending from the beach all the way back into the pathways through the forest. They were playing drums, and the women called out loudly by making the tremolo call of the Indian women.

Chief Thunder Butt stood with Little Hooters at the water's edge. Behind them were over fifty brother warriors, behind them the drummers, and then the women tremolo callers. All the people of the entire village took up the flank, lining the pathways back through the forest.

Melon Dog seemed nervous, frightened by the large, noisy crowd. Running Deer patted his head to reassure him: "You battled a giant croc 100 times your size, but a crowd of friendly, noisy, people scares you? You a strange dog."

We dropped the gangway and tied up the boat. When Melon Dog hopped ashore, Little Hooters ran to him and dropped to her knees. She hugged his neck.

"Who is this friendly fellow?" she asked us with delight.

The chief interrupted the introduction. "Welcome home, warriors! Tonight at the great fire you will tell us the tale of your adventures—but first you will enjoy a welcome home breakfast feast."

"Yum-yum!" cried Jumping Jack.

All the people were very happy to see us, and they marveled at the animals and goods that we had brought to them from Miami in trade for their crafts. The drummers played loudly, and the women tremoloed as the chief led us home. The cheering crowd parted as we walked through the throng of people. Like conquering heroes, we were welcomed home.

Little Hooters walked behind us with Melon Dog at her side. I kept turning to look at her beautiful face and lovely smile. I wanted to take her in my arms, but public displays of affection are not the

Whatchacallit way. Jumping Jack, Running Deer, and Full Moon ignored her, acting like she did not exist, but I knew that they, too, longed to hold her. I know that it is true that

Absence makes the heart grow fonder.

Chapter 14

THE VISION OF SORROW

THURSDAY, NOVEMBER 1ST, 1973

The evening after our return from Miami, the elders honored us with a feast. Drumming, singing, and dancing preceded the feast, and all the goods that we had brought home from Miami were put on display for the people to examine. After the gluttony, my crew and I were asked to describe the adventures and ordeals we had experienced while on our voyage. In turn, we each stood on the talking mound near the fire pit and described our memorable adventures.

First we told the tale of our battle with the pirates, and then of course our encounter with the giant, mutant croc a bull gator. My friends enjoyed telling the people how I had gone loco during the terrible hurricane and hailstorm, and that made the people laugh. The most popular tale was the description of our epic battle with the croc, and the people demanded that the story be repeated over and over. Our tales become more embellished, dramatic, and detailed during each telling, and the people did not tire of our stories.

Because I could not speak the Whatchacallit language well, despite having learned some rudimentary words and phrases, I was the least requested speaker. I believe that the only reason I was asked to speak at all was out of courtesy and politeness. Full Moon was the most popular orator. His descriptions were vivid, and he spoke rapidly and dramatically in the Whatchacallit tongue.

Although I could not understand everything Full Moon said, Jumping Jack told me that Full Moon had a flair for public speaking and that he was prone to excessive exaggeration and embellishments, especially when describing his own bravery and prowess. I noticed him making a lot of eye contact with Little Hooters as he spoke. She politely smiled at him as he puffed out his chest and told his tale.

When Full Moon had finished his version of the events, Chief Thunder Butt rose from his seat holding his scepter and announced that Little Hooters' father, Wise Owl, wished to speak to the people. Wise Owl walked to the top of the speaking mound.

"My daughter Little Hooters has come of age and has many worthy suitors looking upon her. My family is honored to learn that eleven eligible Whatchacallit warriors have asked our elders for permission to look upon my daughter, Little Hooters. She has decided that she will look upon only two of these brave warriors. She has chosen Jumping Jack and Sun Chaser Eddie Ocean. She must decide between these two brave warriors.

"As is the tribal custom, we will consider the offerings that both eligible bachelors bring to my family. Then the two courters will compete for Little Hooters' hand in marriage to determine who is the superior warrior. The warrior games will be held, and the test of strength, speed, and survival skills will commence on the night of the next full moon. [That would be Saturday, November 10th.] Good luck. May the best warrior win my daughter's hand!"

I looked at Jumping Jack, who stood next to me with a stern expression. I asked him what Wise Owl meant about our "offerings to the family." Jumping Jack told me that offerings are a dowry that a man gives to the woman's father as payment for his daughter's hand.

"But I don't have many personal belongings to offer, nothing of much value," I said.

"I feared that you might offer your *Watermelon* boat. All I have to offer Wise Owl are my three longboat canoes and 100 conch shells. *Watermelon* be much better offering," said Jumping Jack.

"But what would I do without my boat—become a farmer?" I asked.

"Wise Owl would keep you as captain. He is the son of Night Owl, the medicine man. Wise Owl is a learned man who will soon become an elder and a wise man. He never be a sailorman," said Jumping Jack.

"Then I guess I will make him that offer," I said.

I was once again amazed by the openness and honesty of my Indian friend. He had offered his honest opinion and advice, even when it was to my advantage and his detriment!

The chief spoke again. He raised his scepter and said, "So be it! After the warrior game challenges, Little Hooters will choose between Jumping Jack and Sun Chaser Eddie Ocean! Now I proclaim the conclusion of these festivities!"

Melon Dog rubbed up against my leg before following Running Deer home to his lodge. Little Hooters smiled at me as she walked past with her parents, and I longed to go with her. Exhausted, I returned alone to the *Watermelon* to sleep and to ponder all that I had just learned about the Whatchacallit tribal customs.

During my sleep, another vivid vision came to me. The face in the glowing light appeared once again beside my hammock where I slept.

"Follow me, Sun Chaser Eddie Ocean. You have failed to understand the gravity of your situation. You did not comprehend your vision into the future, so now you must see a new vision. You must accept and understand what actions to take before it is too late to change your destiny. See this vision. It will reveal the consequences of your life choices."

Enveloped by the light, my spirit rose above the boat. I could see my body asleep in my hammock below. I floated higher with the spirit and came to a pathway through the clouds.

"We are now traveling your life's path. Follow me," said the spirit.

The pathway continued for quite a while, and then we came to a fork, a bifurcation, with one path leading to the left and one path going to the right.

"We are now at the current moment in your life. You stand at a crossroads. You are about to choose a path into your future. A person cannot write his own destiny, but every person's final fate is affected by his life choices. You will now experience a rare blessing—a chance that most people do not receive. You will be shown the consequences resulting from the important decision that you face."

The spirit pointed ahead and said, "Choose a path to follow, and then go."

I chose the path to the left and floated forward, alone. The spirit remained at the fork on the main path. As though watching a time-lapse film projected onto the white bank of clouds, I saw my whole future life flashing rapidly before my eyes. I was married to Little Hooters, and we were very happy. We went on sailing adventures together and returned home to her family often. This vision made me indescribably happy! I could not tell how many years elapsed before the happy vision turned to one of great suffering and sorrow.

In this vision, the spirits called me to service, and I was ordered to conduct a humanitarian mission in Africa. Little Hooters and I made the transatlantic passage safely in the *Watermelon*, but ten days after arriving on the shores of Liberia, Little Hooters fell ill. She asked me to send her back home to be with her mother. She wanted to fly back to Miami on a plane, but I thought she was overreacting, and I took her to a missionary hospital instead.

"You probably just have a case of the flu. You never get sick, Little Hooters. You will be better in no time, and then we will sail home—together," I said to her.

I went off to complete my mission. Two days later I returned, and the English missionaries said that Little Hooters was suffering from the advanced stages of malaria and might not survive. I could not believe what they told me—she was never sick. She begged me to send her home to die with her people, but the doctors told me she would not survive the trip. She had a better chance if they continued treating her, they said.

Even though Little Hooters had a high fever, she shivered and said she was freezing to death. She cried for her family and became delusional. She began speaking to her mother, father, and grandfather, Night Owl, as if they were in the room with her where she lay dying. She was angry with me for taking her so far away from her home and family, but then a moment later she forgave me and apologized for becoming cross. I sat at her bedside and watched helplessly as she suffered both physically and spiritually and died a slow and painful death.

"No! This cannot be our destiny! I refuse this destiny. I defy my destiny!" I returned to the fork in the main path of my life, visibly shaken.

"Spirit! Take me out of this vision! Return me to my bed!" I demanded.

"First you must travel the other path," said the spirit.

"No! I cannot bear it. No more of these visions, please!" I begged.

Against my will I began drifting down the path leading to the right. Once again the rapid film began playing before my eyes. This vision was a rerun, exactly the same as the vision that I had had when I was in Miami. The vision that the spirit said I had not learned from, the vision with Little Hooters and Jumping Jack happily married and playing with their children. Family and friends surrounded the happy couple. The only difference this time was that I saw even deeper into the future. This time I saw Jumping Jack rise to the position of tribal chief, and at the end of the vision the happy couple had aged and were playing with grandchildren. Then it was over, and I was back on the main path with the spirit.

"You have been blessed with this vision by the great Wanaka...the grandfather and God of all the spirits and all the ancients. Wanaka does not want you to suffer; he has given you the rare chance to control your own destiny and the destiny of the woman that you love. Now you must return to your bed, return to your sleep. You must make your own life choices. Make the choice of your own free will."

The vision ended, and I awoke in a sweat, shaking violently. I felt that I had a fever, and I drank a lot of water. It was now clear to me that I must not marry Little Hooters. It would be selfish and unbearable to spend a few happy years with her only to see her suffer and die while still a young woman. With Jumping Jack she would be happy and have a long and healthy life. The choice was obvious; I would have to step aside and let Jumping Jack win Little Hooters' heart.

As the day proceeded, I realized that my queasiness was not being caused by a physical illness; I was suffering from a broken heart. I knew it would be a long time before I would forget the cruel twist of fate that had been revealed to me in my vision of sorrow. It was very hard for me to give up my dream of marrying Little Hooters and to accept my destiny without her.

Dreams die hard!

Chapter 15

THE WARRIOR GAMES

SATURDAY, NOVEMBER 10ᵀᴴ, 1973, 9:00 PM

The autumn night was cool and the humidity low, a welcome relief from the South Florida heat. To the east a full moon, the harvest moon rose in the clear, night sky. The warrior games and my competition with Jumping Jack would commence at sunrise. Earlier in the day, the tribal elders had announced the sequence of the events. On day one, the test of strength and fighting skills would be held, on day two, the test of speed and agility conducted, and day three would begin the test of our survival skills and the game of wits.

The contests were designed by the tribal leaders to help the eligible bride and her family choose her most worthy suitor. The overall winner of the warrior games would also gain high standing with the tribal elders, prestige among his fellow warriors, and the adulation of the entire tribe.

In my vision of sorrow, the spirits had made it clear that I needed to relinquish my quest for Little Hooters' hand in marriage. Only by marrying Jumping Jack would she be spared the horrible fate that had been revealed in the vision of sorrow. I needed to withdraw from the competition or lose the warrior games competition so that Little Hooters would be forded to marry Jumping Jack.

The present dilemma was how best to bow out—withdrawal would be an insult to Little Hooters and a disgrace to my reputation. The least painful solution would be to lose the warrior games to Jumping Jack, which was probably inevitable anyway. My competing and losing would save face for all three of us.

Little Hooters agreed to meet me at the Kissing Place at 9:00 pm. It was 8:50 pm when I heard her humming a tune and walking toward the outcrop of limestone where I waited. The sound of her voice was sweet and beautiful. *Such a sound could only be coming from the voice of an angel*, I thought.

My heart skipped a beat when I saw her walk into the clearing. She wore a tan doeskin dress with black leather stitching. A crown of yellow flowers adorned her head, highlighted by her silky, jet-black hair. She was the most beautiful woman I had ever laid eyes on; she was my soulmate. Again, I could not understand how the great Wanaka could be so cruel. *Why would He prevent us from being together?*

"You look very pretty tonight." I greeted her and hugged her tightly. That sweet fragrance of honeysuckle was on her breath, and I kissed her lips.

"Do you know why I'm the happiest girl in the world? Because you will soon be my husband." She gazed into my eyes, and her smile captivated me.

I wanted to kiss her again, but I pulled back from her, realizing that showing affection would not make our inevitable breakup any easier. It was not fair to show Little Hooters my true passion and desire, because our love could never be fulfilled. Sadness and confusion filled my heart as I struggled to find the strength to end our relationship.

"Little Hooters, you say you want me for a husband, but what about the Warrior Games—the battle? What if I lose? Then you will have to marry Jumping Jack, right?" I asked.

"No! The games are just an ancient tribal custom. The result is not binding. It's just a silly ritual, conducted when a woman has looked upon more than one suitor. If you don't win it does not matter. I have already made up my mind. I have chosen you, Sun Chaser Eddie Ocean! You will be my husband—win or lose."

Losing to Jumping Jack would have been the perfect solution to my dilemma, but the news that the contest was not binding threw a monkey wrench in my plan. Little Hooters was going to choose me, win or lose. Now I was back to square one. I would have to tell her about my vision of sorrow! Somehow I would have to reject Little Hooters outright, but telling her that I did not love her was too cruel for me to imagine.

We walked out to the tip of the point that extended above the water's edge *Now lovers' leap finally makes sense to me!* I thought.

I was ready to tell her about my vision of sorrow, but when she looked into my eyes, I knew I wasn't capable of breaking her heart. Weak and ashamed, I could not muster the courage to tell her that we could never be together. Once again the love sickness was inside my chest, breaking my heart all over again.

"Let's sit down," I said. My legs felt weak as I sat on the split-log bench and looked up into the vast universe.

If I cannot spend my life with Little Hooters, we can at least enjoy this moment. We could spend one last night together. I looked at the moon above and held back the tears that welled in my eyes.

I offered up a silent prayer toward the heavens: "Wanaka, if only you would allow me to be the one who suffers and dies, I would gladly take that fate, that destiny. Just to spend a few precious years as Little Hooters' husband, I would gladly give up my life."

She noticed the sorrow in my eyes. "Why are you sad? Are you worried about the Warrior Games tomorrow—the battle? I told you, it's meaningless to me. Win or lose, nothing changes. We will be together," she said.

After having known this woman, this earth angel, how could I live without her? How could I ever love another woman?

It would have been better for both of us if we had never met! What were the gods thinking? How could they have let our paths cross? Letting us fall in love was not just, not right; it was cruel! My anger toward the great Wanaka grew.

We sat together beneath the pines and talked. Moonlight filtered down through the branches that swayed in the gentle breeze. Little Hooters' beautiful smile was illuminated in the soft moonlight as wispy shadows danced across her face. She spoke to me of her hopes, dreams, and the plans for our future. It was torture for me to hear her dreams of our future together; plans that I knew would never come to fruition. I listened in anguish but forced myself to hear her words so that someday, after she was long gone, I could relive her wonderful plan and our life together, if only in a dream.

"Look! A falling star! Make a wish!" she said as she pointed to the sky.

I made my wish. I wished to stay with Little Hooters; then my bitterness prevailed.

"That's a meteorite, not a falling star. Which reminds me, I have something for you." I reached into my pocket.

"That's a lovely stone, but not very romantic, Sun Chaser Eddie Ocean."

"This is not an ordinary earth stone. This is a piece from what you just saw in the sky. It's from a meteorite—a chondrite to be exact. It was perfectly round, but I had it split in half and strung on this silver chain by a jeweler in Miami. See all the glass beads on the inside surface? The little beads are many billions of years old and are made of the stuff that forms the planets, moons, asteroids, and comets. All the elements of the universe are in that tiny rock."

"Now I see its inner beauty! Look at all the little colorful glass beads inside! It's wonderful! Thank you!" She kissed my cheek.

"It's like you, a little piece of the heavens that fell down to earth. A glowing light in the dark sky, sent to brighten this harsh and bitterly cold world. Also like you, it's beautiful on the inside. How's that for romantic?" I asked.

"Much better. You're learning—but you don't seem yourself tonight. You seem a little cynical. Are you angry about something?" she asked.

"I got that stone from Mr. L. Lucky Bean's catalogue." I ignored her question.

We sat in silence for a while, stargazing, and then at midnight we kissed again. I held her in my arms, wondering if that would be our last kiss and said, "It's midnight, and now we must go. Now we must part." The love sickness filled my chest.

"Yes, for now we part. But don't look so sad, my love. The future will be ours." She smiled, and I could not bear to leave her.

"I'll walk you home." I said.

Unaware of the secret that I kept, she hummed happily as we walked to her home. Her love song ended at the stoop of her parents' lodge. We were now in the public eye, and we could not kiss good-night. Instead, she blew me a kiss and I waved goodbye.

Morning came all too fast. At nine o'clock, three warriors arrived at my boat. They informed me that they had been assigned to be my trainers for the warrior games. They offered me salted fish and venison jerky. I got a can of Kalik ale to wash down the dry, salty food, but they took it away and gave me water instead.

"Bitterroot water no good for training fighters," said Tall Bear. He handed me a buckskin loincloth to wear.

"You must wear traditional loincloth for battle," said a short but heavily muscled fellow named Angry Boar.

I took off my white linen pants and white cotton shirt, and then struggled with the loincloth. The three Indians scrutinized my well-toned but thin, pale body as I changed clothing.

"I suggest you not fight Jumping Jack. Better you raise the hoop of surrender before the fight even starts," said Tall Bear.

"Yes, you not have much chance against Jumping Jack today. Today strength-challenge day. Maybe you have better chance another day," said Crouching Panther.

"That's what I like—coaches who instill confidence," I said sarcastically.

"Not your fault. Jumping Jack be strongest warrior and best grappler in all of tribe," said Tall Bear.

"Thanks—that makes me feel even better. Good job, Coach."

I didn't know if I had any chance of beating Jumping Jack, but I did know that my warrior friends were underestimating my abilities. They were unaware of my past and of my self-defense training among the Wasichu people.

I had grown up on a farm in Kentucky and had been tossing sixty-pound bales of hay, digging holes, shoveling manure, and chopping firewood since I was eight years old. When I was twelve, my family moved near Philadelphia, and I began playing organized sports. At the age of fourteen I tried wrestling and was able to beat kids who had been wrestlers for many years. I was often underestimated due to my unimposing appearance and youthful face. My body was slender, but I had broad shoulders, and I was often told by the city dwellers I was "country strong."

After learning some wrestling moves and techniques, I became more successful at the sport and made the varsity team as a sophomore. As a senior I was named team captain. My college had no sports teams, but as an adult I joined a private karate and jujitsu dojo, learning advanced self-defense techniques.

After arriving in Florida, and while working as a radiographer at Jackson Memorial Hospital, I took up boxing at the Fifth Street Gym on Alton Road in Miami Beach. A trainer named Al Viladari allowed me to spar with some of his professional boxers, and he told me that I was a natural. In 1972, my martial arts training and career as a radiographer both ended when I became a full-time sea captain after buying the *Watermelon*.

Perhaps now you understand why I had confidence in my ability to make a good showing against Jumping Jack. Although my trainers were treating me like a lamb being led to the slaughter, I was sure I could defend myself.

Tall Bear put me through a warm-up drill and a series of calisthenics and then paired me with Crouching Panther for a sparring session.

"Go slow, Panther. No striking. Don't injure Sun Chaser before the warrior games even begin," Tall Bear instructed.

We faced off. Crouching Panther came at me bent over at the waist with arms extended. He grabbed me behind my neck and under my left bicep, a classic wrestling stance. We jostled for position. He was strong and had good balance, but by grabbing his right arm with my left hand and under-hooking his left armpit with my right arm, I was able to pivot my hips and use a judo throw to take him to the ground with a thud. He scrambled and tried to counter my move, but I gained his back and sank in double leg hooks to flatten him out on the ground. He lay face-down, pinned to the ground, as I snaked my right arm under his chin and around his neck. With my rear naked chokehold applied, he was forced to submit. The match was over in less than thirty seconds.

"Whatchacallit! Where did you learn that fighting?" exclaimed Tall Bear.

My three trainers looked at me like I had just dropped in on them from another planet.

"Let's see if you can do that to me, Sun Chaser," said Tall Bear.

Tall Bear was tall and rangy. He used his long reach to strike me with openhanded combinations. I knew that a closed fist would have done considerable damage to my face. I switched to boxing mode and began bobbing and weaving to slip and block his strikes, using footwork that Miami Al had taught me. Because of my much shorter reach, I either kept just out of range or quickly darted in close so that I could land my own open-handed blows.

By the look on Tall Bear's reddened face, I could tell he was surprised and impressed with my boxing skill. He must have expected to run right over me, and he became frustrated. Suddenly, after letting out a wild yelp, he bull-rushed me. I was taken off guard by the sudden explosive move and was knocked to my back.

Tall Bear jumped on me and gained the full mount position. He began striking me with his palm to my face until I grabbed hold of his arm and lifted my legs up and over his head and neck, catching him in a leg triangle. I turned my body sideways and cranked hard, hyper-extending his vulnerable arm. My arm bar applied great pressure to his elbow joint, and with a loud yelp of pain he surrendered, and the match was over.

"Whatchacallit!" Crouching Panther and Angry Boar said in unison.

"We underestimated you! You are ready for the battle, Sun Chaser. You might even have a chance against Jumping Jack after all!" said Tall Bear.

With good sportsmanship and no hard feelings, Tall Bear acknowledged my fighting skills. He smacked me hard on the shoulder, exclaiming, "Whatchacallit!"

"I hate that!" I said as I squeezed my aching shoulder.

It was noon. My trainers announced that it was time to proceed to the arena of combat near the farming village. We jogged at a slow pace and entered the horseshoe-shaped arena just after noon. The arena was a grassy clearing surrounded on three sides by steep, elevated banks of tightly packed crushed shells mixed with sand and clay. People had begun gathering and were sitting on the steep banks. The arena was about the size of a typical high school football stadium. People were eating lunch and playing games, much like tailgaters before an NFL game. Drummers were playing, and people were celebrating in anticipation of the coming battle.

Teenage boys standing in the arena began separating into two groups, half stood in front of the west embankment and half in front of the east embankment. A referee stood in the middle of the grassy field as one boy from each side was led by a trainer onto the field of combat. When the matchup was announced, people flocked to an embankment, either the west side or the east side, to stand behind their preferred fighter.

Conch shells were piled at the foot of each embankment; then the people sat down on the steep hill to cheer for their favorite contestant. I realized that the offering of shells was a form of wagering. In the first battle, the favorite was apparently the boy from the west bank—the pile of shells in front of the west bank was larger than the pile on the east side.

"Who are all these boys? What is the purpose of this contest?" I asked my trainers.

"Some of the older boys wish to be designated as future tribal warriors. They must prove themselves worthy. If successful, they will take the oath of loyalty and become dog soldiers, warriors in training. We will train them. Then, when older, they will become the warriors and guardians of the people," answered Tall Bear.

"What about those very young ones? Some can't be more than eight years old," I asked as I pointed to a pair of little fellows waiting on deck.

"The young fellas have a personal argument to settle. Fighting not be allowed in village. Boys must have permission from the elders to fight. They fight, they settle grudge, then they be friends again. That is the custom," said Tall Bear.

"As a boy, I have many fights! Still I hold the record for most grudge matches," Angry Boar said with pride.

The first match between the two teenage boys was a spirited battle. The referee prevented serious injury by stopping the contest when one combatant began to dominate his opponent. The referee raised a feathered hoop to signal the end of the bout. For my own sake, I was glad to see that these were not brutal battles causing serious injury or death.

The victor in this match was the odds-on favorite from the west embankment. He was hoisted upon shoulders and marched around in front of his cheering fans; he would one day become a warrior. His opponent, although bruised and defeated, seemed proud of his effort.

The people sitting on the east embankment congratulated him for his bravery. Then the shells from the east side were collected and distributed among the people on the west side.

"This is an interesting ritual. But why are all those people sitting on the north bank—in the end zone?" I pointed to the end of the enclosed U-shaped arena, the bottom of the U.

"Those people not pick side, not wager any shells. They be neutral. Some be judges."

The last preliminary bout was decided, and then all the winners gathered together to be honored with a short victory ceremony. Next, Chief Thunder Butt announced the main event, my match versus Jumping Jack.

I saw Little Hooters and her family sitting at the very top of the ridge in the end zone. She smiled and waved to me.

What have I got myself into now? I thought to myself.

I considered taking Tall Bear's advice by walking into the arena and raising the white-feathered hoop of surrender, but forfeiting the match would be a disgrace to me and an insult to Little Hooters and Jumping Jack. Better to suffer a little physical pain than to disgrace myself.

After all,

An injury is sooner forgotten than an insult.

Chapter 16

THE WARRIOR GAMES: DAY ONE

SUNDAY, NOVEMBER 11TH, 1973

I stood with my trainers in the north end of the arena; there was a commotion at the south end, and people began standing to see what was happening. It was Jumping Jack entering the arena. His face had been painted—the war paint depicted yellow thunderbolts striking downward across his cheeks into a blue ocean painted on his jaw line.

He walked tall, his powerful shoulders pushed back and chest puffed out as he came into the clearing and onto the field. His oiled body glistened in the sunlight; the muscles in his thighs bulged with each of his long, confident strides. The people sitting on both embankments greeted him as he walked down the center of the grassy field toward me. They cheered loudly when he gave them the open palm salute, and I realized that in comparison, I had received a rather anemic reception from the crowd. I noticed my trainers staring at me. The look of pity had returned to their eyes.

A young woman tugged at my arm. "I will paint your face now," she said and began dabbing at my face with the end of a pussywillow twig. As she worked on my face, my trainers began smearing my body with a sweet-smelling oil of thin viscosity.

"That smells like coconut and fish," I commented, but my trainers did not respond to my nervous small talk. With a grim expression, Tall Bear led me to the staging area at the enclosed end of the arena. Jumping Jack walked with his trainer to the same area, and we both stood before the chief.

"How does my face look?" I asked Tall Bear, but again my trainers did not respond. They just gazed at my face with a blank stare and then frowned. Later I discovered that a yellow sunburst had been painted on each cheek with the silhouette of my boat, the Watermelon, depicted sailing in front of the setting sun. Like my baby face, the war painting was not very intimidating or inspiring.

The chief spoke through his cone-shaped megaphone. "Jumping Jack, you will now be measured and weighed!"

Jumping Jack stood still with his arms at his sides as a judge used a short stick and an acorn to measure his height. I was familiar with this measuring technique because I had seen fishermen use it to measure the length of large game fish. The stick was about ten inches long and the acorn about one inch.

"Jumping Jack: seven stick, four acorn," said the judge.

I calculated his height: 7x10=70 plus four one-inch acorns would equal seventy-four inches, or six feet two inches tall. Jumping Jack was among the tallest men of the tribe; the average height of the men was about 5'9".

Next, Jumping Jack was led to a long board that was set over a log. It looked like a teeter-totter. He stood atop one end of the board and a man began placing sacks filled with dry beach sand on the other end. When the nineteenth sack was placed, Jumping Jack rose off the ground, and he stood in balance with the sand bags.

"Jumping Jack weighs nineteen sand sacks!" announced the judge.

I had also seen the sacks of sand used to weigh fish, and I knew the sacks weighed about ten pounds each. That meant that Jumping Jack weighed about 190 pounds.

The process was repeated on me. It was announced that I was seven sticks and two acorns tall, and seventeen and a half sacks, which meant that I was six feet tall and weighed 175 pounds. Jumping Jack had a two-inch height and fifteen-pound weight advantage. A murmur spread through the crowd.

"Jumping Jack will defend the west; Sun Chaser Eddie Ocean will defend the east." The chief again spoke loudly into the megaphone.

Many people began scrambling to place conch shells at the foot of the west embankment, and then they jostled to find an open space to sit down on the crowded west slope. Very few people placed shells at the foot of the east embankment, on my side. The spectators finished placing their bets and found a place to sit, and then the trainers led Jumping Jack and me to the center of the grassy arena.

There, a referee waited for us. I recognized him as one of the tribal elders who had opposed accepting me into the Whatchacallit Tribe. I sensed that he did not like me, but I decided not to object to him being the referee because I had yet to see any Whatchacallit person commit an intentional act of injustice.

The old man motioned to us with a large round hoop that was adorned with many white eagle feathers. He used the hoop to direct me to stand with my back to the east bank, and Jumping Jack faced me with his back to the west.

I turned and looked to the east side of the arena and saw my supporters, about twenty people, sitting in a small huddle on the nearly deserted embankment. Among them I saw old man Dancing Bird and the woman who had been given the doe that Running Deer had shot in the dill weed patch. She held her precious little Dill Doe on her lap. Most of the people on my side were from the farming village. I guessed that the farmers might have been supporting me because I had brought them many crop seeds for planting.

There was not enough room on the west bank for the large horde of people supporting Jumping Jack. Hundreds of people spilled over onto the edge of the field of battle.

The referee laid out the rules: "There will be two matches. If you each win one match then we will have a third and deciding match. The match will continue until one man submits or I stop the match to prevent serious injury by raising the feathered hoop of surrender."

Drummers began playing loudly, and women called out with the shrill tremolo call. People rose to their feet, excited with anticipation, and cheered; the sound was deafening and came overwhelmingly from the west embankment. Jumping Jack stood tall; his painted face made him look fierce, and his emotionless expression was frightening. He turned to face the northern embankment of the arena and then raised his right hand in the open palm salute to Little Hooters.

"Hoka hey!" yelled the referee as he brought the hoop down from above his head. This was the command to fight.

We began to circle one another, looking for an opportunity to strike. I remembered that Tall Bear had warned me that the bull rush that he had used to take me to the ground during our training session was one of Jumping Jack's favorite attacks. I braced myself for the charge. Sure enough, Jumping Jack feigned a punch and then charged in for the takedown. Even though I knew the move was coming, I was barely able to defend myself. I felt like a truck was running over me as I dropped down low. I used Jumping Jack's momentum to my advantage by ducking and rolling. I under hooked his left arm so that as I rolled across my back, I tossed him over me, and he landed on his back with me on top.

Jumping Jack began bucking his hips to shake me off. I swung into a side mount position and attempted an arm bar but was amazed to feel myself levitating off the ground and into the air. Jumping Jack had a hand around my throat and one under my thigh as he bench-pressed me above his supine body! Then, while still holding me above his head, he sat upright and in one motion hopped from the sitting position onto his feet. He held me high in the air over his head like I was a rag doll.

"That move was not possible!" I said out loud. I considered the feat of strength that Jumping Jack had just demonstrated to be humanly impossible.

Now I knew how Jumping Jack had been able to send that pirate into a low-altitude orbit when he tossed him off the *Watermelon* He had unnatural strength.

I must have looked ridiculous, thrashing and kicking my legs, suspended above Jumping Jack's head. He paraded me around in front of his adoring fans, and I could hear the people cheering wildly. I tried in vain to get an arm around his neck as he looked at the referee and jerked me in an up-and-down motion, threatening to slam me head-first into the ground. The referee raised the round-feathered hoop high into the air. The hoop was the signal to stop the match in order to prevent a serious injury.

Jumping Jack had defeated me in less than one minute. He dropped me to the ground. Only my pride was injured. I looked toward my supporters. They were politely applauding. I was too embarrassed to look toward Little Hooters.

"The win goes to Jumping Jack!" The referee raised the hoop above Jumping Jack's head and followed him as he paraded, like an angel with a halo, in front of his adoring fans.

Now there was a time-out and a chance for me to regroup. We were allowed to drink water and talk to our trainers to prepare for the second bout.

"Maybe you have chance another day. Go to the referee and raise the hoop—live to fight another day," said Tall Bear.

"Thanks for the vote of confidence and the strategy session, Coach."

Jumping Jack was not using skill and technique; he was simply overpowering my holds with sheer brute strength. His strength was mechanical, like a hydraulic machine, not a mortal human.

"He's too strong. I need to stay out of his clutches. I'll try disco fighting," I said.

"Good luck, Sun Chaser. Maybe you not smart man, but at least you brave man," said Angry Boar.

We were called back to the field of battle.

"Hoka hey!" the referee commanded.

Once again we began circling one another. Jumping Jack charged me again. This time instead of engaging him I stepped to the side like a matador parrying a charging bull. With my cape-less right arm extended to the side, I hooked his waist as he bull-rushed past. I grabbed his right arm and held it high with my left hand to prevent him from getting a hold on me. His forward momentum spun both of us around three times. Then I released him. As he twirled, I stepped back and delivered a hard, high, round kick to the side of his head. He was stunned momentarily, and the crowd went silent as Jumping Jack staggered but did not fall.

The crowd began cheering again as Jumping Jack shook the cobwebs from his head and began coming at me in the wrestler's stance. I wanted no part of that grappling action.

"The disco fighting is working! Disco him!" Tall Bear yelled to me over the crowd noise.

I began rotating my hands rapidly around one another in front of me, like the paddle on a riverboat—actually more of a Motown move than disco. To counter my attack, Jumping Jack clasped his hands together in front of himself with elbows lifted and extended to the side, and began making a wavelike motion with his arms, a classic disco defense. My rotating hand attack was deflected by his arm-wave defense, and he tried to grab a hold of me. Just in time to avoid his grasp, I did a butt-drop by throwing my legs forward and dropping to a sitting position.

Immediately after hitting the ground, I bounced off my buttocks and back into a standing position. My butt-bounce move evaded Jumping Jack's attempt to grab me, and he came up with only a handful of air. I landed a hard punch to his nose, and he was bloodied and enraged. He began swinging at me with wild roundhouse punches that were easy to avoid. He became frustrated at his inability to connect, and I landed a few quick, short punches to his jaw.

Suddenly he bent low at the waist, let out a yelp, and charged me. I was waiting for him to try that bull-rush again. This time I met him head-on and leaped up into the air, landing on the back of his shoulders as he charged forward. Reaching over the back of his head, I got my arm around his throat and, with my legs, put a scissor lock around his body.

Now I had Jumping Jack in a tight guillotine chokehold. He dove forward, slamming me back-first into the ground, but he couldn't break my grip. I squeezed until my arms ached with fatigue, and finally I felt Jumping Jack going limp. The referee saw that Jumping Jack was losing consciousness, and he raised the feathered hoop. In just over three minutes, I had choked out the mighty Jumping Jack to win the second bout.

Most of the crowd stood in stunned silence and disbelief. I heard muffled cheering from the small group of people on the east embankment. I looked to the north embankment and saw Little Hooters jumping up and down and waving her arms at me until her father ordered her to stop.

The referee raised the feathered hoop and placed it above my head. "The winner is Sun Chaser Eddie Ocean! We will now have a third match to determine the champion of Day One!"

After a short intermission, Jumping Jack and I faced off in the center of the arena for the third and deciding match. The referee held the feathered hoop high overhead and then dropped it down and called out, "Hoka hey!"

Again we circled one another, looking for an opportunity to attack. I must have gained Jumping Jack's respect because he was now being much more cautious, no longer trying to walk right over me. He threw a series of high round kicks and tried a spinning back fist strike, but I was able to slip or block each attempt. I could feel the power behind his blows and did not want to get caught by one of those haymakers.

He threw out his right leg to deliver a straight front kick, and I caught his heel with my left hand. I lifted his leg up high, and Jumping Jack was forced off balance. He hopped around on his left leg as I raised his trapped right leg. He had excellent balance, and I could not get him to the ground. He kept hopping even as I lifted his leg high over my head.

Finally, I was able to trip his left leg in mid-hop, and we both went to the ground. I tried applying an arm bar, but he powered right through my hold and started to stand up. Luckily, I was able to get behind him and sink in double leg hooks, but I couldn't stop him from standing upright. Now I was on his back, riding him around the arena. I didn't know if he was fooling around to entertain the crowd or if he had lost his mind, but he began running and bucking while making snorting noises.

Suddenly he stopped and threw himself backward, slamming my back hard into the ground under the full weight of his body. This maneuver momentarily knocked the wind out of me, and I gasped for air as I switched my leg hooks into a figure-four body triangle. Jumping Jack rolled to his stomach, trying to shake me off, but I followed him, still riding his back and clinging for dear life.

Jumping Jack was in danger of being caught in the same hold that I had used to finish off Crouching Panther during our training session. He thrashed and rocked from side to side, trying to throw me off his back and escape my hold as I regained my breath. Jumping Jack's superior strength and power was being negated by my jujitsu, and I could feel him tiring.

Breathing hard, he finally made a mistake when he lifted his chin off his chest and exposed his neck. I clamped down hard with my leg hold and then slipped my right arm under his chin and around his throat. With his neck in the crook of my right elbow, I clasped my hands and applied the rear naked chokehold. Again I felt Jumping Jack go limp, and I looked up at the referee to see if he would raise the hoop to end the match, but he did not.

"He's out!" I yelled to the referee.

I was in danger of killing Jumping Jack, so I released him and stood up. Jumping Jack lay face down in the grass, unconscious. The referee stood over him. "Get up and fight!" the referee ordered Jumping Jack.

"He's out! Why didn't you raise the hoop?"

I was afraid that Jumping Jack was seriously injured.

Jumping Jack didn't respond when I leaned down and shook him. I couldn't see him breathing, so I turned him onto his back and knelt beside him to listen for a heartbeat. The crowd was silent.

Little Hooters came charging across the field, followed by her great-grandfather Night Owl. She knocked me to the ground, pushing me away from Jumping Jack. Little Hooters gave Jumping Jack mouth-to-mouth resuscitation as Night Owl pressed on his chest. Finally Jumping Jack coughed and started swinging his arms at Little Hooters until he recognized her face and smiled.

"Where did you come from?" he asked.

She kissed him and began to cry.

"I thought you were dead! I've never been so scared!" she said as she hugged Jumping Jack.

"Why didn't you stop the match?" I yelled at the referee, who stood over Jumping Jack, looking at him with a befuddled expression. The old man looked at me as a sheepish grin spread across his face.

"Maybe you wanted Jumping Jack to win, but you almost got him killed! If you weren't so old, I would...." I struggled to regain my composure.

The chief came waddling onto the field and spoke to the referee. "I think you had a wager—a wager on Jumping Jack! Give me the hoop. You no longer referee!" declared Chief Thunder Butt as he snatched the hoop from the old man's hand.

Jumping Jack recovered his senses and asked what had happened. The chief told Jumping Jack that he had been losing the match but that the referee would not stop the fight, and that I had stopped fighting before the hoop of surrender was raised to end the match.

People on the west embankment began demanding that Jumping Jack be declared the victor.

"Sun Chaser forfeited the match! Sun Chaser no fight. Sun Chaser quit!"

"Jumping Jack brave! Jumping Jack not quit like Sun Chaser Eddie Ocean! Sun Chaser not winner! We want rematch!" they demanded.

Little Hooters faced the angry crowd.

"Sun Chaser stopped choking Jumping Jack because he loves Jumping Jack, just as much as I do!"

Jumping Jack asked the chief to give him the feathered hoop. He raised the hoop above his head, and the crowd began to cheer.

"Yes! Jumping Jack winner! Hoka hey!" a man called from the crowd.

But the cheering crowd fell silent once more as Jumping Jack walked toward me and held the hoop over my head.

The chief placed his hand on the hoop as well, and together they held the feathered hoop over my head as the chief announced, "The winner of Day One is Sun Chaser Eddie Ocean!"

Most of the people were stunned and looked at one another in disbelief. My small group of supporters began jumping up and down and cheering, and Dill Doe's mother let out a shrill tremolo call. The farmers had just come into a windfall profit, a wealth of conch shells. They began dividing among them the huge pile of conch shells that had been wagered on Jumping Jack.

Little Hooters stood between Jumping Jack and me with an arm around each of our waists. The chief awarded me a medallion carved from a deer antler. The pendant was strung on a woven, intertwined leather necklace, and they put it around my neck. Then the chief spoke to the crowd in the Whatchacallit tongue.

"What did the chief say?" I asked Little Hooters.

"The chief just told the people that your victory should be an example for the Whatchacallit warriors and all the people of the tribe. He told us that

It's not the size of the man in the fight that counts; it's the size of the fight in the man.

Against the odds, I had not only lived to fight another day, I had won!

The gods must truly be watching over me! I thought to myself as the three of us walked arm in arm from the arena.

Chapter 17

THE WARRIOR GAMES: DAY TWO

SUNDAY, NOVEMBER 11TH, 1973, 8:00 PM

After my victory over Jumping Jack, I asked Little Hooters to meet me at the Kissing Place after dark. I could no longer delay telling her that I could not and would not marry her. She needed to know about my vision of sorrow and the horrible fate that awaited her if we were to marry.

A cold front was pushing down from the north, and the evening was dark and dreary. So was my mood. I stood in the cold rain for over an hour, but Little Hooters did not arrive, and finally I decided to leave. On the path home I found Little Hummingbird walking toward the Kissing Place.

"Hey, Little Hummer, what are you doing here?"

"Little Hooters asked me to come in her place. Her parents have forbidden her to see you until after the warrior games are over," said Little Hummingbird.

"Thanks for coming. I was very worried about her."

"Little Hooters' parents are very upset that Little Hooters favors you over Jumping Jack. Her parents favor Jumping Jack."

"That's no secret. They already treat Jumping Jack like their son—the son that they never had," I said.

"After you defeated Jumping Jack, Little Hooters' mother cried, and her father was angry because Little Hooters was happy that you were the victor. That is why he is keeping you apart."

"If her parents knew the reason that I wanted to meet Little Hooters tonight, they would have gladly sent her to see me," I said.

"Well, I just came to tell you that she is OK but will not be coming. Now I must get home. I'm freezing!" said Little Hummingbird.

"I'll walk you."

I didn't blame Little Hooters' parents for wanting Jumping Jack as their son in-law. He was not only a fierce warrior but also a kind and honorable man. In my vision, I saw that he would someday become chief of the tribe, and Little Hooters would be his queen. Dejected, I went to the *Watermelon* and slept below deck to keep out of the cold rain.

MONDAY, NOVEMBER 12TH, 1973, 9:00 AM

Day two of the warrior games involved a test of speed, agility, and endurance. On several occasions, Jumping Jack had proven to me that he was the faster runner. The most recent had been when the croc a bull gator chased us across Crocodile Island. That day I could not keep pace with Jumping Jack. Unlike fighting, where skill and technique can overcome an opponent's superior size and strength, there is no substitute for speed. Training can improve a runner's performance, but sheer speed is a natural ability that cannot be taught.

The ground was wet from the rainy night, and the morning sky was still overcast. I ate breakfast and had begun doing stretching exercises on the deck of the *Watermelon* when my trainers arrived at 9:00 am.

"Good morning, champ! You are the talk of the village! People cannot believe that you defeated Jumping Jack yesterday! Some think that the witch—Weeping Willow—cast a spell in your favor," Tall Bear called to me from the shore.

"I fear that even Weeping Willow will not be able to help me with today's challenge of speed," I said as I walked down the gang-way and onto the beach.

Tall Bear explained the day's coming events to me. He told me that the first race would be a sprint covering the length of the arena, similar to a 100-yard dash. Then we would run a shorter race, about fifty yards, over four-foot-high hurdles. The grand finale was a long-distance run around the perimeter of all four Whatchacallit villages. The distance race would start and finish in the central village and would cover a distance of over twelve miles, essentially a half marathon race.

"If Jumping Jack wins the first two races, will we still need to run that marathon race?" I asked. I did not think I had much of a chance in the short races.

"Yes, the games are entertainment for the people. The people will be placing wagers. You must try to win the final race even if you lose the first two," said Crouching Panther.

We arrived at the arena by noon. Just like on day one, many young people were preparing to compete in preliminary competitions.

"I see girls are here. Will they compete with the boys?" I asked.

"Yes. Young girls may compete in the running events. The challenge of speed is open to all children under the age of thirteen summers," Tall Bear said.

"Little Hooters won the sprint race three years in a row. She beat all the boys her age until Running Deer beat her the year when she turned thirteen," Angry Boar said.

I looked at the crowd gathered in the end zone on the north embankment and saw Little Hooters sitting between her parents. All three had sullen expressions, and I sensed that the family had been quarreling. I knew I was most likely the cause of their grief.

The children's preliminary races did not include the long-distance event, and the short races were completed in just over an hour. Afterward, a ceremony was held to honor the winners, and then the trainers led Jumping Jack and me to the open end of the arena. I noticed that Jumping Jack had two black eyes, a result of my punches. I wondered if I had broken his nose.

Once again I was assigned to represent the east bank and Jumping Jack the west. I had many more supporters this time, but Jumping Jack still had far more people backing him. We faced each other at the starting line.

"You took me by surprise yesterday. You will not be so lucky today, my friend," Jumping Jack warned me.

"Runners, get ready!" A new referee, a good-natured, elderly man, whom I recognized but did not know, held the feathered hoop high overhead.

"Hoka hey!" he brought the hoop down, signaling the start of the race.

Jumping Jack's prediction was correct—the first race was no contest. He crossed the finish line five yards ahead of me, and the large crowd on the west embankment went berserk! I saw Little Hooters' parents hugging as she sat glumly looking at the ground.

"The winner is Jumping Jack!" The chief announced through his megaphone as the referee held the hoop above his head. The people from the west side gathered the conch shells that my supporters on the east embankment had wagered on me.

Next, four-foot-high hurdles constructed from bamboo poles were set up on the grassy field, ten hurdles in each lane. The distance from start to finish was over fifty yards, about half the distance of the first race. After a fifteen-minute break we were led to the starting line. A light, misty rain began falling again as we stood at the starting line.

"Hoka hey!" Down came the hoop adorned with white egret feathers, and off we went.

We ran at full speed toward the first hurdle, and I timed my stride perfectly and made the jump. After clearing the first three hurdles, I was surprised to find myself keeping pace with Jumping

Jack. Now, with six hurdles behind us we were still neck and neck as we raced to the finish line! With only two hurdles left, Jumping Jack began inching ahead of me, but I still had a chance to win! I tried to stride longer to gain more speed as I leaped over the final hurdle.

Stretching out as much as possible, I flew over the final hurdle, but when I landed my right heel slid on the slick, wet grass, causing my right leg to shoot forward and out from under me. Water sprayed out from both sides of my butt as I went skidding across the finish line a full yard behind Jumping Jack.

The crowd on the west bank roared their approval, and then loud laughter began replacing their cheers as I lay supine in a large, muddy puddle, looking up at the sky with my loincloth up around my neck. Jumping Jack walked over and helped me get up. He could not keep himself from laughing as he yanked me to my feet. My face and hair were covered with brown mud. "That some bad finish, Sun Chaser!" he said.

Children began running onto the field and sliding across the wet grass on their butts.

"Look! I Sun Chaser!" The kid mocking me slid on his buttocks through a deep puddle, spraying muddy water into the air. I recognized him as one of the youngsters who had tried to "borrow" the *Watermelon*. Other children began copying him by running full speed and then sliding on their butts.

"I Sun Chaser Eddie Ocean!"

Now my humiliation was complete! I looked up to where Little Hooters sat and saw her and her parents also laughing at the children's antics and me as I pulled my loincloth into place.

Well, at least I got them to lighten up a bit, I thought to myself.

"Jumping Jack is winner of the first two races! Jumping Jack is champion of challenge day two! We now have a tie. Each warrior has won one day of events. The overall victor will be decided by the survival game of wits, starting on day three of the warrior games!" This time the chief held the feathered hoop over Jumping Jack's head as the crowd cheered their hero.

"But first, we must complete the distance race. The endurance of our two fine young warriors will be tested today."

The chief made his announcement, and all the people began leaving the arena and walking toward the central village, where the starting line for the marathon had been established.

After a twenty-minute rest, we began the long-distance run. Yellow strings tied to trees and bushes marked the route and paths that we were to follow. The race course led from the central village down to the beach, winding through the fishing village, then turned west past the hunters' lodges, and then north, circling the farmers' vast fields before finally returning to the central lodge and the start/finish line. Even though this race did not have an impact on the day's final result, I was going to try to win for the benefit of the people wagering shells on me.

"Hoka hey!" The referee sent us off.

Right from the start, Jumping Jack began building a commanding lead. I lost sight of him after we exited the fishing village, where many supporters lined the path and were cheering him onward. The people of Jumping Jack's home village politely voiced encouragement as I passed by, so I picked up my pace but conceded that Jumping Jack probably had already won this meaningless race. Jumping Jack was far ahead and out of sight.

At the halfway mark, near the hunters' village, I saw Jumping Jack running up ahead of me. He seemed to be slowing, and I was steadily gaining ground on him until he looked back and saw me coming. He kicked it into another gear and was able to maintain his lead, but at least now he was within my sight.

We were running across the onion field in the farming village, three-quarters of the way through the race, when I sensed that something was wrong with Jumping Jack. He was spitting as he ran, and he seemed to be slowing down. Once again I was gaining ground and caught up to him on the final leg back to the central village.

As I ran past, I could see that it was blood that he was spitting. Blood was running from his nose and mouth, and he labored to keep up his speed. His broken nose was bleeding so heavily that it impaired his ability to breathe. He slowed to a jog, and so did I, to allow him catch up to me. We jogged side by side toward the central village and the finish line.

"You're injured! Let's call it a draw. Let's walk together to the finish!" I said.

"No! I will not quit! I will not stop running! You must not quit either. You're a Whatchacallit warrior, Sun Chaser! Don't disgrace yourself or me by quitting! If you can win, then you must win," he said before spitting out a large quantity of blood.

Jumping Jack suffered greatly, struggling to breathe as he ran, but through sheer will power he continued to push on despite the race having no meaning. I resumed running and, to the great surprise of most of the people, I ran into the central village and crossed the finish line first. Jumping Jack bravely finished about five minutes later. There was no doubt that without the broken nose Jumping Jack would have easily won the endurance race.

There was no pity for Jumping Jack from me, only great admiration. I knew fate would make him the winner in the end. Destiny would pair him with the woman of my dreams, the woman I loved, but I was angry with the gods, not with Jumping Jack. I cursed the great Wanaka for not allowing my hopes and dreams to be fulfilled and envied my brave friend and his future with Little Hooters by his side.

Fortune favors the brave.

Chapter 18

THE SURVIVAL GAME OF WITS

MONDAY, NOVEMBER 13TH, 1973, 8:00 PM

I had been victorious on day one of the Warrior Games, and Jumping Jack was the winner on day two. Now the survival game of wits on day three would break the tie and determine the overall champion.

At 8:00 pm on the evening of my loss to Jumping Jack, I walked toward the central village. The tribe was holding yet another feast, preceded by an elaborate ceremony at the fire pit outside the entrance to the grand meeting lodge. This time, the purpose of the festivities was to honor Mother Nature and all the creatures living in the Whatchacallit kingdom.

The tribe regularly gave thanks to the animals that had sacrificed themselves to the tribe's hunters, but each year on this day the ceremony to honor them was elaborate. The Native Americans believed that the spirits of the animals that nourished the tribe now dwelled in the Valley of Tranquility. The people of the tribe hoped to summon those spirits to join them at the tribal celebration.

As usual, the chief provided us with a fine feast. When the last hog rib was tossed onto the bone pile, Jumping Jack and I were asked to join the chief and a group of elders who were sitting in an area known as the sacred circle. The sacred circle is normally reserved for only the holy men and the chief; it was considered a great honor and privilege to be allowed to sit among them.

Together with these holy men, Jumping Jack and I watched as many people, dressed in various animal costumes, danced around the fire pit to the beat of the drums. As they circled the fire, the dancers mimicked the movements of the animals that they represented.

"Now, you must smoke from the sacred pipe of vision." Chief Thunder Butt handed me a pipe that had been crafted from the hollow, long bone of an animal. Colorful pictures depicting many of the indigenous animals had been painted on the pipe, and two large heron feathers hung below the mouthpiece.

I inhaled from the pipe. The harsh smoke was unpleasant and made me cough. I was glad to hand the pipe to Jumping Jack. The pipe was passed around to each elder in the circle, and then it was refilled and passed around once more.

"What did you put into the sacred pipe?" I asked Night Owl.

"Strong medicine—very strong medicine! It is the milk-oil of the giant bufo toad."

I knew that the bufo toad was poisonous, and that when threatened it would puff up its body and secrete a milky white poison from its skin. The toxic smoke from the burning oil made me feel dizzy, and my vision became blurry. The people dancing around the fire began to look like actual animals, not humans. A man dressed up as an eagle appeared to levitate off the ground and take flight over the fire as he flapped his long wings to the drumbeat.

The chief spoke to the crowd through his megaphone.

"Weeping Willow will now call the spirits from the afterlife. She will invite the animal spirits from the Valley of Tranquility to join us at our fire."

The drumming stopped, and the sudden silence hurt my ears. It was deafening. I had a strange feeling of anxiety and covered my ears with my hands. The people dressed as animals stopped dancing and sat down on the ground, facing the fire. They stared into the bright flames as the witch woman, Weeping Willow, walked up onto the speaking mound.

With her arms raised and outstretched toward the sky, she began chanting words in the Whatchacallit tongue. I uncovered my ears to listen. My total immersion with the tribe had helped me to start to learn their language, and I understood that she was casting a spell to conjure up the animal spirits from the afterlife.

Night Owl, the medicine man, spoke to Jumping Jack and me. "Now your awareness is heightened. Now you should be planning your strategy for the coming game of survival. The animal spirits will soon begin showing themselves to you. As you watch them, you must plan your strategy for tomorrow's game."

Night Owl handed the pipe to me. "Smoke more. Smoke more from the sacred pipe of vision."

My body felt strange, and I did not want to smoke anymore, but I did, for I did not want to offend the elders. The pipe was passed around the sacred circle again.

Squinting my blurry eyes, I pointed above the fire pit and leaned over toward Jumping Jack. I whispered to him, "Do you see that? What are those things?"

Embers rose above the fire and floated skyward. Where the embers vanished into the night sky, many small, glowing puffs of smoke began to form. I saw eyes peering out from each of the small, illuminated clouds. One pair of green eyes looked like the eyes of a big cat, a panther. That cloud floated down toward me until it was very close to my face. The eyes of the large predator examined me closely and with curiosity. The eyes frightened me.

"Hoka hey!" I yelled to scare the cat eyes away.

The glowing cloud slowly drifted toward Jumping Jack and stopped just inches from his face. The green eyes of the cat closely examined his features. Jumping Jack was braver than I; he showed no fear and did not flinch.

Now another set of eyes came near my face. These were large, round eyes, like the eyes of a deer. These eyes were kind and were comforting to me. Eyes of many different shapes, sizes, and colors gazed down upon us from a hundred glowing nebulas that floated in a circle above us. The elders seemed to be in a hypnotic trance as they joyously gazed up at the beautiful eyes circling above. They raised their arms and began singing a song of praise, giving thanks to the visiting animal spirits.

Then I noticed something that struck fear into my heart. Hovering above the fire I saw a misty black nebula forming. It contained a familiar pair of eyes. The hideous, evil eyes of hatred glowed red and stared directly at me. Those were the eyes of the mutant crocodile bull alligator. The red eyes began floating downward toward me. My own eyes could no longer focus properly, and my head was spinning.

I must have passed out at that point because when I woke, the ceremony had ended and most of the people had gone home. I got up off the ground and walked home with a splitting headache, contemplating what I had just experienced. The evil, red eyes haunted me as I walked alone in the dark. I imagined that the croc a bull gator was hiding behind every bush along the narrow, dark pathway.

Thankfully, I made it home and quickly fell asleep on the deck of the *Watermelon*.

TUESDAY, NOVEMBER 13TH, 1973, 8:00 AM

I awoke and momentarily didn't know where I was; my head was throbbing. Then I remembered the animal eyes and began trying to determine if the apparitions I had witnessed at the fire pit were real or only figments of my imagination, images conjured up in a disturbing nightmare after I had passed out. I determined that when the animal spirits appeared, I had not been unconscious, so the vision could not have been a dream. I wondered if the toxic smoke from the elders' pipe had caused me to have hallucinations. My questions were answered when Tall Bear, who had not smoked from the sacred vision pipe, arrived at my boat.

"Good sunrise today, Sun Chaser! That was some heap good show the animal spirits give last night!" he called to me from the beach.

"You too, Tall Bear? You saw those floating clouds with the animal eyes?" I was relieved. If Tall Bear had seen them, then that meant that I was not hallucinating and not going insane. They were real!

"Of course. All the people saw the animal spirits. They were making strong medicine! All night they make strong medicine. I not sleep much. The animal spirits are excited about the survival game. You play game today. We must go!"

Tall Bear walked with me back to the grand meeting lodge in the central village. We arrived at 10:05 am. The large edifice was constructed of bamboo poles and cypress wood. In the middle of the massive room was a large, round mat made of interwoven palm fronds. Many people had already arrived to watch the beginning of the survival game of wits. People were sitting in the elevated bleachers and in the upper loft section overlooking the circular meeting hall.

Weeping Willow and Night Owl entered the room. Weeping Willow carried two large parchments made from the bark of the melaleuca, the paper tree. She placed the documents in the middle of the mat. Then Weeping Willow took a crystal ball from her magic bag and placed it on top of the parchments like a paperweight. It was the same crystal that she had been gazing into when she was captured in the laughing trance, the same magic crystal that had been formed from lightning striking beach sand, turning it to molten glass and then cooling and hardening into the crystal ball.

Night Owl spoke. "These are your maps. Each map contains the clues that will lead you to your destination. You must complete your tasks and then return to the meeting lodge no later than noon of the third day, or you will be disqualified! The warrior who returns home first after solving the riddles will be the grand champion of the war-rior challenge games.

"These are the only weapons that you will be permitted to carry." Night Owl placed two large buck knives on top of the parchments.

Weeping Willow sat and gazed into the magic crystal and then spoke. "The crystal reveals to me many things—but not the winner of the game. The winner will be determined by the decisions that you each make. I can see the dangers you face." The witch woman's eyes shifted from the crystal to me.

"I see that you will need this, Sun Chaser Eddie Ocean." She reached into her bag and took out a small vial containing a liquid and handed it to me.

"What is this for?" I asked her.

"Sun Chaser must find the answers himself. I can provide no more help. Jumping Jack, you will need this." She took a round wooden container from her bag and gave it to Jumping Jack. He opened it and sniffed the contents. I could not tell by his reaction if he knew what the ointment inside the container was for.

Night Owl picked up both parchments and stood before Jumping Jack and me. He extended his arms toward us, one parchment in each hand, and then dropped them. The maps fluttered and drifted down, landing at our feet.

"You must each take the parchment that has landed the closest to your feet." Night Owl pointed to the ground in front of us.

We picked up the maps and began reading them. I saw arrows directing me to take a path that I knew led farther inland toward the hunters' village.

I realized that the survival game of wits was similar to a three-day-long scavenger hunt covering over fifty miles of treacherous swampland and forest.

"Now you must take your survival knives and go!" Night Owl gave the command to begin the three-day challenge, the survival game of wits.

In a hurried frenzy, I ran out the door and was about to start down the path toward the hunters' village when I saw Jumping Jack running in the opposite direction toward the beach. I noticed the big buck knife tucked into the waistband of his loincloth, and I realized that I had not picked up my knife. I ran back into the meeting lodge to retrieve it.

When I tried to come to a sudden stop on the palm frond mat, it flew out from under me. Like riding a magic flying carpet, I skittered across the floor and crashed into some clay pots. Once again I found myself lying on my back, this time in shards of broken clay, with my loincloth up around my neck. People laughed hysterically at my bungling start to the challenge, but many cheered me on as I recovered and ran from the hall with my buck knife.

A journey of a thousand steps begins with one first step.

In this case, a misstep!

Chapter 19

THE FORBIDDEN GARDEN

My anticipation was finally over. The survival game was underway! My map directed me to the site of a remote hunting camp located in the southeast sector of the Whatchacallit Empire. The Whatchacallit men slept in this camp when hunting for alligators and hogs deep inside the Everglades. The map indicated the location of a boat ramp on the bank of Alligator Creek, near the camp. After a one-hour jog down a narrow trail through dense woods, I found the campsite but did not see Alligator Creek.

Surrounding me was a dense jungle. I turned the map sideways to figure out which direction to travel as the calls, chirps, and squawks of thousands of birds living in the secluded forest beckoned me. After cutting through the heavy brush and moving about fifty yards east, I heard the trickling sound of water. Because the loud calls of mocking birds, blue jays, big black crows, and cardinals, and the sound of giant woodpeckers hammering on rotted dead wood filled the air, I had to concentrate hard to determine which direction the trickling sound was coming from.

The trickling sound seemed to be located farther east, and it led me to a clearing in the heavy brush. A pathway to the boat ramp had been cut through the brush and buttonwood trees, and I found a narrow but deep creek, Alligator Creek. Six canoes were stacked on two racks along the bank of the creek, and a tree stump offered me an inviting seat to rest upon for a moment to catch my breath. Further examination of the map indicated many land crossings that I would have to make on my journey. Solid lines always indicated routes traversing dry land, and water courses were designated by dotted lines.

At the land crossings I would need to carry or drag my boat over dry ground or very shallow water, so I chose a small, lightweight dugout canoe from the assortment of boats. A long paddle would help me to propel my craft through the water.

Because the bark parchment paper, was so fragile, I decided to memorize the route depicted on my map before continuing the journey. The map directed me to an island deep inside the Everglades swamp. A large X drawn over the oval-shaped, inland island was captioned "Forbidden Island," my final destination.

I needed to enter the Everglades by traveling the length of Alligator Creek, all the way up to Long Lake, where I would find the mouth of Crocodile Creek. Then Crocodile Creek would take me even farther inland to Cuthbert Lake, and at the northeast end of that lake I was to follow an unnamed canal leading to Forbidden Island.

With the route memorized, I began to disembark from the boat ramp but stopped paddling when I saw Running Deer come jogging toward me, shouting. "Wait! Sun Chaser! Take this push pole with you. You will need it to get through the thick reeds and lily pads." He picked up a long pole that was lying next to the canoes. The pole had a "foot" at the end that gave it the shape of the letter L.

"Thanks, my friend!" I took the pole and began pushing off from the shoreline and into the narrow, winding creek.

"Turn it the other way!" Running Deer instructed me to put the end of the pole with the foot down into the water, not above my hands.

I tried poling the canoe in that manner. "Thanks...that works better." The foot kept the pole from sinking deep into the soft bottom of the creek and propelled the boat faster and with less effort.

"Good luck, friend." Running Deer held his right hand up, palm out, the Indians' salutation of both greeting and farewell.

Never before had I ventured westward into the vast Everglades swamp. It was exciting to explore such a foreign place. Poling the sleek canoe up the winding creek against a gentle current was nearly effortless. The water was clear and clean, not the muddy swamp water that I had expected to find.

As I progressed deeper, I was amazed at the beauty of the place. Tree branches covered with hundreds of exotic orchids arched over me as I passed through the colorful tunnel of flowers. Bees busily buzzed overhead, and the birds continued to sing.

Soon, the trees became so dense that I could not stand upright in the canoe due to the low-hanging branches weighted down with the fat, colorful-tongued orchids. I sat down and used the long paddle to propel the canoe.

The map indicated that I was approaching the head of Long Lake, where Alligator Creek originated. Upon reaching that point, the water widened, and I entered the lake. Now miles of sawgrass were visible, extending as far as the horizon. Here and there, dotting the sea of grass, were clumps of tree-covered islands.

Above me, clear blue sky replaced the shady canopy of flower-covered trees, and the sun became hot. Many pretty water lilies with flowers of various colors lined the shoreline of the wide lake. I imagined Little Hooters with one of the yellow lily flowers in her hair, and that helped take my mind off my thirst.

I could sure use an ice cold Kalik.

I had just begun my journey, and I was already thirsty and hungry. Not having a supply of fresh water worried me. The lake water was crystal clear, and I considered drinking from it but resisted for fear of getting dysentery, a condition that could be fatal to a person all alone in the swamp. Beyond the water lilies lining the bank of the lake, the sawgrass grew six feet tall in shallow water and formed an impenetrable barrier to both man and beast. I imagined that only birds and the smallest of fish could pass that way.

I continued north, and off to my right I saw a sizable clump of dense bushes and small buttonwood trees rising above the tall sawgrass. Many birds of different species were perched throughout the foliage. It was a rookery. Noisy mother birds sat in nests. Most of the birds were white, but a spattering of colorful plumage made the view spectacular.

There was a large patch of dry land about three acres in size beneath the foliage of this rookery, a large oasis in the sea of razor-leaf sawgrass. This island would be a perfect spot in which to camp for the night, but I decided that it was too early in the afternoon to end the day, especially without food or water. Paddling north on Long Lake, I continued to admire the landscape.

"Mother Nature, I had no idea of the beauty you were hiding out here in your Everglades! Now if you could only provide me with a little water, I would be most grateful and love you even more!" I spoke out loud.

The Everglades were not the ugly, muddy swamp that I had expected.

Up ahead and to my right there was a disturbance on the surface of the lake, and I paddled toward it to investigate. It was a deepwater spring, an upwelling of clean, fresh water through the filtering, porous limestone, emerging from the depths and bubbling to the surface. From cupped hands, I drank in much of the cool, fresh spring water. Splashing the chilly water all over my head gave me some relief from the blazing sun. A hog bladder was rolled up in the bow of the boat, and I filled it with spring water. Obtaining potable water relieved my greatest worry: dying of thirst. I could go for days without food if necessary, but water was essential.

Thank you, Mother Nature! Thank you for your blessing, was my silent prayer of thanks. Now well hydrated, I continued on my northbound course.

Midway up Long Lake, off my starboard beam, I found Crocodile Creek. I turned the little boat to the right and entered the mouth of the creek. Once again I was paddling beneath a beautiful canopy of orchid-covered tree branches lining the shore. Many alligators were sunning on the banks of the deep creek, and I wondered if the waterway had been misnamed, or if crocs did live in this fresh water. The alligators scurried off the shoreline and dove into the water as I approached them. I prayed that there were no giant, mutant crocodile bull alligators living out here.

After about thirty minutes, the creek opened into Cuthbert Lake. This lake was much wider than Long Lake. My map directed me to navigate toward the northwest shore of this lake and enter an unnamed waterway that would lead me deep into the heart of the expansive Everglades and to the shore of Forbidden Island.

When I reached the north end of the lake, I discovered a small peninsula of land jutting off the shoreline. It was a patch of high, dry ground about an acre in size. I pulled over there; it was my last chance to stop before entering mile upon mile of sawgrass plains. I went ashore and began setting up camp for the night. I collected thin, soft, green branches and piled them high beneath two large coco plum bushes; the branch pile would be my bed. Then I wedged the small canoe upside-down above the bed in the branches of the coco plum bushes. The canoe formed a roof over my head.

Next I scoured the area to see if there was a source of food. On the west side of the little peninsula I found many ripe paw-paw fruit. Paw-paw is like a wild papaya, only much smaller than a papaya. I also found a tree loaded with ripe guavas. These fruits, combined, made a simple but satisfying fruit salad dinner.

By the time I had finished eating, the sun had set, and I lay down, exhausted, upon my bed of branches. I rested peacefully, surprised that no mosquitoes were tormenting me. Even though it was nearly the winter, the shorelines of Florida were infested with mosquitoes, but here, deep in the Everglades, I had not received one bite.

I was sleeping for a few hours before I awoke to the sound of varmints fighting and scurrying around in the underbrush. I decided that they were probably rats, coons, or opossums feeding on the guavas and that they posed no threat to me. I ignored them and went back to sleep. Then at about two o'clock in the morning, I awoke again, this time to the sound of thunder. I was glad that I had used the canoe for shelter because heavy rain came, and I heard water trickling as it ran along the ground beneath my elevated bed. The storm was short lived, and I slept snugly in my little bird's-nest bed.

WEDNESDAY NOVEMBER 14TH, 1973, 7:00 AM

The morning came, and I awoke refreshed and eager to continue my journey. I realized that today was my twenty-first birthday, and I ate a few more guavas to celebrate. Under the guava tree, I noticed animal tracks. My hunch had been correct. Rat and coon tracks covered the ground. I was glad that no gators had come up from the water to hunt the varmints and found me asleep in my nest, as I would surely have been a much larger and more satisfying midnight snack.

I launched the canoe and continued traveling up the north bank of the lake. Barely half a mile from my campsite, I found the unnamed waterway shown on my map. The waterway was a natural deep channel running due north through the thick sawgrass. For five hours, I paddled and poled but saw nothing but many more miles of sawgrass extending all the way to the horizon in every direction.

Finally, at about 3:00 pm, trees were visible ahead of me, but they were still far in the distance. By poling hard and picking up my pace, I reached the island in less than an hour. Many large trees covered the island, rising high above the sawgrass. The map indicated that this was my final destination—I had arrived at Forbidden Island.

I stopped fifty yards off the bank to see if it was safe to go ashore. The place not only looked peaceful, it was beautiful, a paradise of fruits and flowers. But something was not right; even though the place was isolated, far from civilization, nothing appeared to be growing wild. The grounds and foliage looked like they had been meticulously landscaped and well maintained. I wondered if there were humans living here. With caution, I slowly poled toward the gorgeous, forbidden botanical garden.

After landing the canoe, I pulled it up onto the bank and secured the bow line to a tree. My treasure map indicated that I needed to find seven odd-looking gold nuggets that were covered with little spikes, and also something that looked like the severed head of a reptile. For me to win the survival game, I needed to collect these objects and bring them back to the central meeting lodge before noontime the next day.

With the long push pole and my knife, I headed inland but did not get far before I was brought to a sudden stop. Directly in front of me was a ditch full of angry snakes. They were large water moccasins. I walked along the length of the ditch to find a way around it but soon realized that the ditch was actually a moat that encircled the entire island.

There must be a way over or through this snake pit.

I reached into the pocket on the inside of my loincloth and took out the tube of liquid that Weeping Willow had given to me.

This liquid must be antivenin to use for a snake bite, I surmised.

I prayed that I would not have to use the antivenin and walked along the moat until I found a narrow section. Then I went back and retrieved the canoe and pushed it into the moat. It slid over some snakes, but the angry water moccasins did not retreat; they threatened me by opening their jaws wide and exposed long fangs protruding from gaping, cotton-white mouths.

"That's why we call you cottonmouths, you nasty little devils." The sound of my voice made the snakes even angrier, and they struck out at the canoe, making a drumming sound on the hull as their fangs bounced off the cedar wood.

The length of the little canoe reached only halfway across the ditch, and the water was only a few inches deep, not enough to float my boat. I got in and tried to pole forward, but I was grounded in soft mud. By walking to the bow of the canoe, I determined that the boat was just long enough to allow me to leap from the bow to the opposite bank. After looking at the intertwined, spaghetti mass of poisonous snakes, I knew that if I miscalculated the distance of the jump, or that if I were to slip, I was a goner, so after taking a deep breath I jumped above and over a dozen cottonmouths.

They uncoiled and struck upward at me like unleashed springs. One very large snake reached me, and its fangs nicked the great toe on my left foot but did not penetrate or inject the deadly venom. I was left with a long, superficial scratch on the side of my great toe. Armed with my long push pole and my knife, I continued traveling inland and entered a bountiful garden of indescribable beauty!

"All of this fruit among these beautiful flowers! I will have a wonderful supper tonight!"

I was speaking to a mango tree and was about to pick the largest and most perfectly ripe red-yellow-green mango that I had ever seen until Weeping Willow's words filled my head: "Do not partake of the Forbidden Fruit!"

The voice startled me, and I pulled my hand back from the fruit. A gentle breeze stroked and ruffled my long hair, sending the scent of every irresistible fruit and flower on the island into my nostrils. The unearthly aromas tempted me and enveloped me all at once; they were irresistible, and my stomach ached with hunger as I fought hard to resist the seductive redolence.

With great effort, I resisted my hunger pangs and looked at the map to distract my attention from the tempting fruits hanging just inches above my head. The picture of the severed reptile head and the odd, golden objects drew my attention. I needed to find these things, pronto, and bring them home.

Well, it's clear—the reptile head must represent a water moccasin. I'll cut one's head off on my way out of here, no problem, but what are these seven golden nuggets? I wondered.

I proceeded farther inland, searching for the gold nuggets. Again, I was stopped in my tracks, this time by a loud sizzling sound. At first I thought it was the sound of a thousand cicadas, but it was different. Another mass of snakes, thousand of snakes, lining an incline in front of me was the source of the noise. This time the varmints were eastern diamondback rattlesnakes, and they were raising hell with their rattles as they coiled and stood their ground, inflamed by the sight of me. Just like the moat full of water moccasins, the rattlers imposed a defensive ring around the top of the island. They occupied the entire incline encircling the peak and highest point of Forbidden Island.

I approached the dreaded reptiles with my long push pole extended in front of me. I probed and prodded the pit vipers; they did not retreat. Even when I crushed the head of a snake beneath the foot on my push pole, they stood their ground. As I crushed the skull of a second snake, others struck at the pole, marring it with small nicks, and venom dripped off the end.

I began lifting the rattlesnakes off the ground with the L-shaped end of the push pole and tossing them right and left, clearing a path through the deadly rattlers. Unlike the water moccasins, the rattlesnakes did not aggressively attack me; they stood their ground but did not come after me. I was able to work my way through their ranks and reach the peak of the island.

Thank you, Running Deer! Thank you for telling me to take this push pole with me. I did not know how I could have gotten through that gauntlet of snakes without that long pole.

Now I stood at the peak of Forbidden Island, and in the center of the Forbidden Garden. Below, I surveyed the expansive, immaculate garden and could not believe that a more beautiful place existed on earth. It was literally paradise! I could not travel farther inland; I had reached the epicenter of the place but had not found the golden nuggets.

At the very peak of the island, a tall, unusual tree with a spiraling, corkscrew-shaped trunk grew. The tree was the crown jewel atop the Forbidden Garden. While standing beneath the tree, I noticed human bones scattered about the ground and counted fourteen human skulls among the bones.

You guys must not have had any antivenin. Again I touched the vial of liquid beside my left hip.

Something in the branches of the tree caught my eye and caused me to gasp. "Whatchacallit! There they are! The golden nuggets!" I shouted with joy.

Hanging off the tree branches were hundreds of large, golden fruits with spiked skins. They were the size of watermelons. The drawings on the map were not nuggets at all; they were these unusual fruits. I had never seen such a perfect and beautifully colored fruit before. The closest thing to them that I had ever seen was a big jackfruit being sold at a Miami greenmarket.

I started to climb the tree to collect seven of the golden fruits, but when I grabbed the trunk of the tree preparing to shimmy up, it came to life! The trunk of the tree moved beneath my hands! Then I felt a searing pain in my right thigh. Looking down, I saw the massive head of a snake biting into my thigh. The head was as large in diameter as my chest. The serpent had been coiled around the trunk of the tree, perfectly camouflaged; even now it was barely distinguishable from the tree trunk.

"Hoka hey!" I yelled, more out of fear and surprise than bravado, as I reached for my knife.

Before I could draw my weapon, the serpent uncoiled from the tree and whipped itself around me. Then it slithered slowly across me, inch by inch tightening the noose that was its powerful body. My arms were trapped at my sides as the serpent squeezed harder. I recognized the creature as a giant anaconda, a snake that kills its prey by constriction. Every time I exhaled, the snake tightened its coil, preventing me from inhaling oxygen. I was being crushed and suffocated. I could not move, and I could barely breathe.

A coil of the snake's body was just below my jaw. Tilting my head down, I bit the snake hard. I kept biting and twisting my head from side to side, trying to rip flesh from its body. The snake did not like me biting back, and he released my thigh from his jaws. That is the good news; the bad news is that he took a bite hold on the top of my head. His fangless teeth were short and raspy, designed for latching onto and holding his prey as he squeezed the life out of the victim. Once the victim was dead, the snake swallowed his meal whole.

I was horrified to feel the giant anaconda unhinge his jaw and begin to move his mouth over my head and down my face. The pointy, raspy little teeth drew blood from my scalp. Blood ran into my eyes. I prayed for a quick death as I felt the sticky mucosa of his mouth on my face and smelled the musky stench of the reptile's foul breath.

My entire head was inside the creature! I was being eaten alive. Everything went black as my head started to slide down the snake's slimy gullet, and his jaws moved over my shoulders. I prayed for death and thankfully, I felt unconsciousness coming.

Just as I felt about to pass out, I felt a crack and a pop on my left hip. I imagined my pelvis breaking and the bone shards puncturing my skin as I felt a warm liquid—surely my blood—spreading over my hip and thigh. How ironic for me to die so young and on this day, the day of my twenty-first birthday. I needed one more breath to survive for another minute. I gasped, trying to suck in air, but no oxygen was left.

Then, suddenly, I saw the face of my dead father in the darkness. "Do not give up, son!" I heard my father's plea.

Suddenly the snake spit me out! I gasped for air as the sudden brightness of daylight blinded me. The snake uncoiled itself from my body and began thrashing about as I lay limp on the ground. I touched my left hip to see if it was broken, but it seemed fine. I felt only fragments of the broken tube that contained the liquid antivenin.

Shakily, I got to my feet and saw the huge snake violently thrashing and spinning over and over along the ground. It moved spastically and wildly like the little red wiggler earthworms that I used for fishing bait when I was a young boy living in Kentucky.

Smoke was coming off the serpent's body, and I saw deep burns in its flesh. It looked as if someone had doused the anaconda with sulfuric acid. I touched the fluid soaking my hip and thigh, and it didn't burn me—in fact, the liquid was soothing and gave my skin a pleasant, tingling sensation.

Antivenin wouldn't react like sulfuric acid on the snake—and sulfuric acid would have burned me just as badly as it did the snake! That liquid was not antivenin, and it wasn't acid, either. It was something else. Maybe something magical—something that the witch woman, Weeping Willow, concocted. I finished my thoughts and recovered from the shock of having been nearly eaten alive.

The anaconda lay quivering on the ground, near death. Cautiously, I approached the beast and kicked it hard. It didn't respond. Now I realized that the anaconda's head was most likely the reptile head depicted on my treasure map. It was the severed head that I needed to bring home with me. I drew my knife and then hacked off the head of the giant anaconda.

Apparently the giant snake had not learned the old adage,

Keep your head in a crisis!

Chapter 20

ESCAPE FROM THE FORBIDDEN GARDEN

The severed head of the giant anaconda was stuck like a pike onto the foot of my push pole, which was leaning up against the golden fruit tree. The large, golden fruits hanging above me were out of my reach, so once again I prepared to climb the mysterious tree. But this time, before climbing, I scrutinized the tree trunk and its branches, looking for more hidden dangers. Nothing in the tree looked unusual, so I leaped high and grabbed the lowest branch. Like a gymnast on the high bars, I pulled myself up into the tree and climbed toward the nearest fruit. In short order, I had collected the required seven golden fruits.

Each watermelon-sized fruit was a handful to carry; they weighed about twenty pounds.

"How am I to transport these heavy, oval fruits through the twin gauntlets of deadly snakes?

By cradling a fruit in the crook of my left arm, I was able to carry my push pole in my right hand. The giant anaconda head was still spiked securely on the foot of the pole as I walked toward the ring of rattlesnakes. Stopping four feet from the snake-infested incline, I set the first golden fruit on the ground. I needed both hands free in order to clear a path through the snakes. I tried to shake the snakehead off the push pole, and the head popped off the pole, bounced once, and then rolled down the incline and into the pack of rattlesnakes. The anaconda head looked like an oversized bowling ball as it rolled down the slope.

To my amazement, the rattlesnakes didn't strike out at the anaconda's head. In fact, they fled from its path. The severed head came to rest at the bottom of the incline, and all the rattlesnakes slithered away from the earth that was bloodied by the giant serpent head. Like the Red Sea parting before Moses, the snakes opened a wide path for me to walk through, unscathed. I picked up the first fruit and walked to my next obstacle, the ditch full of water moccasins.

Now the second gauntlet of vipers, the moat full of water moccasins, stood in my way. Wondering if the moccasins would react the same way as the rattlers had when confronted by the giant anaconda head, I stuck the head back onto the foot of the push pole and extended it toward the aggressive snakes. At first they opened their white, cotton mouths wide and bared long, venomous fangs. Several moved toward the severed head to attack it—but then suddenly they stopped. They closed their mouths and remained very still as they rapidly flicked their forked tongues in and out. The wispy, long tongues, detected the scent of the giant anaconda, and they wanted no part of him.

Just like the rattlers, the moccasins also fled in fear, opening a wide path for me to walk through. Walking without fear, I made it to the canoe and put the first golden fruit into the boat. With the aid of the anaconda's severed head, I was able to carry all seven of the golden fruits past the vipers and load them into my canoe. I tied the big anaconda head to the bow of my little canoe, and now the little boat reminded me of an ancient Viking ship with its prow adorned with a ghoulish dragon figurehead. By tying a bowline knot around my waist, I was able to drag the heavily loaded boat over the land and toward the water. My long journey home had just begun.

My task was complete, but now I was in a race against the clock. I needed to make it back to the central meeting lodge before high noon the next day, November 15th. Under the unforgiving heat of the South Florida sun, I poled and paddled as fast I could. My goal that day was to make it all the way back to Long Lake and the bird rookery island before nightfall. By leaving the rookery island at sunrise, I would have a good chance of finish the final leg home before high noon.

In order to keep up a consistent and steady pace, I sang a tune as I poled and paddled the boat. By late afternoon, I was reaching the point of exhaustion. The sun was low in the western sky, and I had run out of water. I knew that I was becoming dehydrated.

My hope dwindled as I continued onward. Then, to my great relief, I saw the deep-water spring bubbling to the surface of Long Lake just yards ahead of me. Hurriedly, I drank from the spring and then filled the water bladder. There was no time to waste, no time to rest.

It was nearly dark when I pulled the canoe ashore at Rookery Island. Many birds had already roosted, nested down for the night. They did not appreciate the disturbance caused by my arrival. The birds squawked and screamed loudly and angrily at me, but I was too tired to pay them any mind. Since it was now too dark to try to set up a decent campsite, I simply set a few of the fruits on the ground to make enough space in the bottom of the canoe for me to lie down. Exhausted, I quickly fell into a deep sleep.

After a few hours I woke when large, wet drops splashed down on my face. Another unwelcome shower had awakened me. The large droplets plopped on my face and wet my hair and body. I felt groggy, and every muscle in my body ached from my long day of frantic poling and paddling. It took me a few moments to clear my head, and I realized that the shower I was receiving was not rain. I was being covered with bird droppings. The slimy white guano covered the canoe, the golden fruits, and me.

My eyes had become acclimated to the darkness, and I could see hundreds of roosting birds above me. Every once in a while a fowl's smelly, digested seafood dinner would come squirting from its butt and rain down on me! I had been so exhausted that I had slept through hours of this offensive mizzling! The foul, fowl, fecal sludge was an inch deep in the bottom of my canoe, and my hair was muddy with the odorous white slime.

I looked for an open space that did not have a canopy of trees above and found only one small, open spot nearby. I dragged the boat to that area but was too tired to worry about my stinky, slimy condition and once again fell into a deep sleep.

It was about 3:00 am when the squealing scream of an animal interrupted my sleep. Startled, I grabbed the knife from my hip and stood up in the canoe. Near the water's edge a raccoon was spinning in a circle as if it were chasing its own tail and screeching loudly.

It must be rabid...hope it doesn't see me.

I cowered down in the canoe and watched the coon. The critter did not appear to be in pain or distress of any kind—in fact, it seemed to be playful and euphoric, but crazed with ecstasy! I had never seen such a thing before and did not know what to make of the coon's behavior. Suddenly, the raccoon dropped to its side and lay motionless on the bank.

Slowly, I approached the raccoon and, with my long push pole, I prodded the animal. He was dead; he had just suddenly keeled over and dropped dead! Not knowing if the coon was diseased, I left him where he lay and got back in my bed of bird crap, attempting to get more sleep.

It was less than an hour before I was once again awakened. This time it was a splashing noise that woke me. I looked toward the water and saw a small alligator snatch the raccoon carcass off the shore before submerging with it into the black water.

Less than five minutes later the alligator was spinning, splashing, and thrashing at the surface. The thrashing lasted for several minutes before the gator became still, rolled onto its back, and floated upside-down on the surface of Long Lake, dead! I did not know what to make of the strange night I was having on Rookery Island, but I had only about one hour left to rest.

THURSDAY, NOVEMBER 15TH, 1973

I woke just before sunrise. My wish that the previous night's shit shower had been just a bad nightmare went un-granted. I reeked of the white slime that had now dried and hardened in my hair and on the boat. The giant, severed anaconda's head on the bow of my canoe looked like the head of a ghost snake, painted white by the bird droppings.

I prepared to depart by loading the golden fruits back into the canoe and noticed that one fruit had been bitten into, and some of the flesh had been eaten. It looked like the work of a raccoon, and I wondered if this golden fruit was the cause of the raccoon's crazy behavior and death. Then the alligator ate the coon, and it also died! Could these golden fruits be so toxic, so poisonous that if eaten the toxin could kill? Kill animals right up the food chain?

Thank you, Weeping Willow! Thank you for warning me not to eat from the Forbidden Garden!

I did not have any time to wash or groom myself; this would be a race right down to the wire. It would take a small miracle for me to make it home before the noontime deadline. I pushed off from the shore and into the lake as a thousand birds mocked and laughed at my messy condition. With loud screams, squawks and calls, they taunted their unwelcomed guest as I departed.

I imagined the birds saying to me, "Good morning. Did you have trouble sleeping? You look all pooped out! Caw! Caw! Caw!"

"You dirty birds sure look much prettier when viewed from afar!" I called out to my warbling tormentors.

I couldn't get away from Rookery Island fast enough! The beginning of what I knew would be another day of exhausting, frantic paddling under the blazing Florida sun had just begun. With the light of the morning sun, I got a clear look at what a mess the seabirds had made of the boat and me. I considered diving overboard to rinse my hair but knew that these waters were infested with gators and maybe crocs, and I had no time to spare. I paddled the canoe furiously, purposely splashing water onto the boat and over myself. The rinse did very little to wash away the dried, white bird crap. No need to worry now, I thought, because later,

It will all come out in the wash!

Chapter 21

A RACE TO THE FINISH

B y the height of the sun, low on the horizon, I estimated that it was close to 6:30 am when I left Rookery Island. That gave me less than six hours to make it home to the central meeting lodge and across the finish line. Failing to make it in time would disqualify me from the survival game competition, and all my hardships would have been in vain.

Paddling hard, I began to sing the song that Mick had written for my friend. "Jumping Jack is a gas, gas, gas!" Singing helped me keep a steady rhythm and pace while I paddled.

I paddled through the flowery tunnel of foliage covering Alligator Creek, but this time I had no time to stop and smell the roses.

My trip down the winding creeks and across the two broad lakes was uneventful. Finally, at about 10:00 am, I beached the canoe on the boat landing next to the hunters' camp. Now I had to figure out a way to transport the seven giant golden fruits back to the central village. Each melon-sized fruit weighed over twenty pounds, and the severed anaconda head added another fifteen pounds to my load. The total weight was over 150 pounds.

I considered dragging the loaded canoe by the bow rope, but it was too heavy. Then I recalled how in Miami, my Indian friends had used pony drags to haul our goods to the trading post. I decided that a pony drag would solve my problem. We had constructed the drags out of a tarp and a couple of 2x4 boards. I needed to find similar items now.

I used my long push pole and another that I found on the ground in front of the canoe rack. Then I discovered a cast net draped over the canoes. By tying the fishing net between the two push poles, I made a nice pony drag. Eight miles of land separated me from the finish line.

After I loaded the golden fruits into my pony drag, Melon Dog arrived and began barking loudly. The dog's barking alerted Running Deer and the other hunters of my arrival. They came to the boat landing to see what the commotion was all about.

"Hey, hey, Sun Chaser! You survived! You made it back. Now you must hurry to the finish. Your time is running out!"

Running Deer smacked my weary shoulder. "Whatchacallit! If you hurry, you can make it, Sun Chaser!"

I could barely talk due to exhaustion and dehydration. "Give me a drink," I whispered in a raspy voice.

I drank from Running Deer's gourd of cool water and then grabbed the ends of the two push poles. I placed the ends of the poles with the feet under my armpits and began to jog home, pulling the pony drag behind me. Melon Dog ran ahead of me, barking encouragement and leading the way home.

Running Deer told me that a large crowd had been gathering at the finish line since sunrise. They had come to witness the finish of the warrior game survival race. People speculated, wondering if there might be a winner this year. In the past, competitors had had less than a fifty percent success rate at finishing the survival challenge on time. In fact, one quarter of the warriors attempting the challenge never returned home at all, and their bodies were never found.

A crowd gathered near a long string that was strung chest high across the main path and tied between two palm trees. The string designated the finish line. Jumping Jack would be coming into the village from the west and I would be arriving at the finish line from the east. People began placing conch shells as wagers on either the east side or the west side, depending on whom they favored in the race.

I ran past the hunters' village, dragging my heavy load down the sand and shell pathway, gasping for air. The relentless sun was taking a toll on my body as I struggled to keep a steady pace. About a mile from the finish, I slowed to a walk and staggered forward. I felt faint and could not continue. Defeated, I began to sit down in the middle of the path, but Melon Dog began barking at me again. I must have been delirious from dehydration and exhaustion, because I could hear the dog speaking to me. Inside my head, I heard the dog encouraging me to not give up. Somehow, he was communicating with me, but the voice in my head sounded like my own voice, as if my thoughts were a translation of the dog's barking.

"Keep going, Sun Chaser Eddie Ocean! You are almost home now. You can do it. Follow me!"

Three times the dog ran up to me where I sat and then turned to run away down the pathway toward home. He was encouraging me to get up and follow him. He barked loudly. "Follow me!" Again I heard him speak to me with *my* voice, inside my head.

Semi-consciously, I struggled to my feet and started a slow and painful jog, hoping that I would not faint. I followed the pesky little collie down the path.

I entered the outskirts of the central village at 11:50 am to a cheering crowd, which lined the main pathway. The world was spinning out of control in front of me, and the distorted faces of people called out, but the only sound I heard was a loud buzzing in my ears. People were cheering me onward, and even though I could barely understand them, I thought I heard a few of the spectators telling me that I had lost the contest.

"You did not make it! You have lost to Jumping Jack!" I seemed to hear a man say to me as I passed close to him.

I was barely jogging when I stumbled across the finish line at 11:57 am, only three minutes ahead of the 12:00 noon deadline. The string that designated the finish line was already broken and lying on the ground. After walking over the string, I fell forward on my face and collapsed in a heap.

People dowsed me and the forbidden fruits with buckets of cool water and then they rinsed the bird poop from the anaconda's head.

"Look! He has the forbidden fruits! Is that a giant snake head?"

People gathered around me and examined the unusual cargo in my pony drag as they gave me water to drink. After several minutes, I was able to stand and began to regain my senses. A large crowd was gathered in front of Night Owl's medicine hut.

"What is going on over there?" I asked in a parched, raspy whisper.

"Jumping Jack is there. He finished the race ten minutes ago, ahead of you, Sun Chaser—but he is in very bad condition. A Wanton wasp stung him. Night Owl said a man could die from such a sting! Night Owl and Little Hooters are trying to save Jumping Jack's life."

"What is a Wanton wasp?" I asked the man.

"They are giant wasps that live only on Wanton Island. They are wasps as big as that dog!" The man pointed at Melon Dog

"They are nasty demons! Jumping Jack needed to steal their honey to win the survival game. Wanton wasp got Jumping Jack good. Wasp sting Jumping Jack on back, but Jumping Jack not quit! Jumping Jack win survival game, but now he might not survive!"

Painfully, I slowly walked to the medicine hut but was not allowed to go inside. Outside the entrance to the hut I saw a small tub containing large chunks of honeycomb wax dripping with golden honey.

"Is that the honey? Is that what Jumping Jack was ordered to bring home? Those Wanton wasps must be giant honeybees, not wasps," I said.

"I saw the Wanton wasps once. Never want to see again! They not bees. They have long, ugly wasp bodies, but they make honey, like honeybees. They be giant mutant bee-wasps—only live on Wanton Island. Never want to go there—never again!" an elderly man tried to explain.

I heard the chief calling all the people to come to the central meeting lodge. Once the crowd had gathered around the speaking mound, the chief announced that Jumping Jack had won the warrior game of survival.

"Jumping Jack has won two out of the three warrior game challenges! Therefore Jumping Jack is the grand champion of the warrior games!"

The chief motioned for me to come up to the mound. He commended me for putting forth my best effort and for performing very well in the warrior games. He raised his scepter above my head, and I bowed.

"Sun Chaser Eddie Ocean has competed hard and brought great honor to himself and the Whatchacallit tribe. He has brought home seven forbidden fruits and the head of the great serpent that guards Forbidden Island. He is the first warrior in eight years to return from Forbidden Island. Fourteen brave warriors went there and have never returned. This is the head of the great devil serpent."

The chief held the severed anaconda head high for all to see. The people cheered loudly. "Hoka hey! Hoka hey! Sun Chaser Eddie Ocean! Hoka hey!" they chanted, and then the chief continued speaking.

"Sun Chaser Eddie Ocean did not fail. He finished his quest with only minutes to spare, but a superior warrior, Jumping Jack, beat him by over ten minutes. The elders will recommend that Little Hooters and her family choose Jumping Jack to be Little Hooters' husband."

189

The compassionate chief looked at me with kind, empathetic eyes. I was not disappointed that Jumping Jack would be the chosen one. Days earlier my fate of being a lone sailor on the vast sea had been revealed to me in the vision of sorrow.

"Jumping Jack is in very bad condition. Night Owl has removed a six-inch-long barbed stinger from the warrior's back. The Wanton wasp's stinger narrowly missed Jumping Jack's spinal cord, and the venom has left him unable to move his legs. We hope this is a temporary condition. It is a miracle that he was able to make it home before his legs became paralyzed by the venom."

The chief raised his scepter to the heavens to give thanks. "Tonight's closing ceremonial feast will be postponed. We will postpone the celebration until Jumping Jack has recovered and is able to attend the feast."

The crowd groaned with disappointment as the chief made that announcement.

"This concludes the warrior game challenges. Hoka hey to Jumping Jack, our new champion!"

On the way home to the *Watermelon*, I stopped by the medicine hut to inquire about Jumping Jack. Little Hooters and Jumping Jack's parents were mulling around outside. They said they had heard nothing new about Jumping Jack's condition, so I walked home with Melon Dog at my heels. Once we were away from the village, I stopped and turned around to ask the dog, "Did you talk to me, or was I delirious, crazed by thirst and exhaustion?"

The dog barked three times, and I imagined I heard him saying, "Yes, you heard me talking to you, just as you hear me now! You are a stubborn man, but you finally opened your mind to your sixth sense."

I wondered; *Could this be possible? Had I been given the Indians' gift, the ability to communicate with animals?*

"No, that is not possible! This is spooky—I must be losing my mind! Those dang Indians have me talking with animals now!"

I was still in denial but was also excited at the possibility that the voice in my head was actually Melon Dog communicating with me.

The dog barked twice this time, and I swore I heard him saying, "Eventually you will accept the fact that you are communicating with me, because,

Sooner or later, every dog has its say!

Chapter 22

THE SIXTH SENSE

I staggered back to the *Watermelon* exhausted; my entire body ached. Onboard, I collapsed onto the deck. Melon Dog lay down beside me, and I fell asleep at 4:00 pm. I slept all afternoon and through the night. I did not wake until after 3:00 pm on Saturday.

SATURDAY, NOVEMBER 17TH, 1973

Although I had eaten very little food for two days during the survival challenge, I was not hungry, but my thirst was insatiable. I could not drink enough water to quench my thirst.

"Let's get some grub."

The voice surprised me. I looked to the beach but didn't see anyone. Melon Dog sat in front of me, staring attentively into my eyes.

The dog barked once. "I'm starving!" The voice was coming from inside my head!

Talking out loud to myself, I said, "I must have suffered brain damage from the anaconda attack. I experienced a lack of oxygen, and now I'm hearing voices inside my head. I have suffered brain damage."

The dog barked twice. "When are you going to believe it is me that you are finally hearing? You don't have brain damage. You're just a stubborn dimwit."

Melon Dog sat rigidly upright, attentively staring at me. I tried to ignore his eerie gaze and averted my eyes from his haunting stare.

"Let's see if we can find you some grub around here!" The voice would not shut up!

I went below deck to get away from the dog's intense stare.

The dog barked excitedly. "Now that's more like it! Lets get some grub from the mess deck!" The pesky collie followed me below deck.

I fed Melon Dog. The food diverted his attention from me. He gobbled down the salty fish jerky and sloppily lapped up water from his bowl. Thankfully, the voices in my head ceased jabbering at me, and I regained my composure.

"The voices of insanity are giving me a moment of peace!" I said to the dog. I was not yet ready to acknowledge an ability to communicate with animals.

"I'm going to the medicine hut to check on Jumping Jack. You stay here and guard the boat," I said to the dog. He was too busy eating and drinking to pester me now.

At Night Owl's hut, I found Weeping Willow standing outside, holding her magic bag. She was casting a spell of good health for Jumping Jack. I waited until she finished her incantation, and then I asked her, "How is Jumping Jack doing? Is he any better?"

"His life is out of danger. He will live. But Night Owl is worried about his leg paralysis, worried about his spine," she said.

"Jumping Jack is stronger than an ox. He will be walking in no time. He will recover," I said with confidence.

I knew this was true because I had seen Jumping Jack's future in my vision. I had seen Jumping Jack as tribal chief.

I looked at Weeping Willow's magic bag, the bag from which the mysterious vial containing the liquid that had killed the anaconda snake had come.

"Weeping Willow, I need to ask you, what was that acid that you took from your bag and gave to me? The acid in the vial—it saved my life. It burned the giant anaconda but had no effect on me! How was that possible—for the acid to not burn me?"

Weeping Willow explained, "That was not acid. The night before the warrior games began, the ancients living in the Great Teepee called me to the Valley of Tranquility. I traveled to them in a vision. I was given that vial of liquid in the vision."

She looked toward the sky and closed her eyes, momentarily embracing the wonderful memory of being in the Meadow of Tranquility, and then continued. "The ancients told me that the liquid—the liquid inside the vial—was the tears of the Great Wanaka. The liquid was His tears of sorrow. His sorrow for all the many lost souls that aimlessly wander the earth without faith. Sorrow for the evil forces that freely roam every corner of His creation and corrupt mankind."

"The tears of Wanaka? You mean the tears of God? I carried the tears of God with me? Why did His tears not burn me, not burn my flesh as they burned the serpent?" I asked.

"The tears of Wanaka did not harm you because you are not an evil man. If you had been a man of bad intentions, the tears would have killed you—just as they killed the evil serpent."

Still looking up to the sky, she began another chant, another incantation.

I heard a voice speaking to me. "Did you come here to see Jumping Jack?"

Little Hooters was standing in the doorway to the medicine hut. She looked a mess and no longer had the sweet aroma of honeysuckle. She was disheveled and exhausted from lack of sleep and worry. She had been caring for Jumping Jack day and night.

"Yes! Thank you! I would love to see him," I said.

I had never seen Little Hooters look so bad. I was concerned for her health as well. "How are you holding up, Little Hooters?" I asked.

She broke down and began to cry. I hugged her, and her tears wet my shoulder.

"He can't move his legs! Can you imagine Jumping Jack...?" She couldn't finish the sentence and began sobbing uncontrollably.

"He is going to be fine. Nothing stops Jumping Jack." I tried to comfort her and kissed her forehead.

She remained outside to regain her composure before going back to Jumping Jack's side. After entering the medicine hut, I did not even recognize Jumping Jack. He lay supine in the bed, staring at the ceiling with wide, sunken, black, hollow eyes. His skin was gray and greasy-wet. He did not notice me for a minute, and I was too shocked by his condition to speak. Little Hooters came into the hut, and Jumping Jack must have sensed our presence; he turned his head and smiled when he saw me.

"I kicked your butt, brother!" He spoke in a weak voice, a whisper.

"I want a rematch—as soon as you get your lazy ass out of bed!" I said as I hugged him tightly.

He was very embarrassed by my embrace in front of Little Hooters. He tried to push me away, but he was too weak.

"Little Hooters, Sun Chaser Eddie Ocean is going soft on us. Maybe he not strong enough to be warrior man." Finally he weakly pushed me away.

"Well, good! You're regaining some strength!" said Little Hooters as she put a rolled-up blanket under his knees.

Night Owl came out of the back room. "OK, now let Jumping Jack rest. Come back tomorrow, Sun Chaser."

The grizzled old medicine man waved me out the door, and Little Hooters followed me outside. Weeping Willow was still there, reciting incantations, so I could not talk openly with Little Hooters.

"We need to talk. Meet me at the Kissing Place tonight," I whispered.

After dark I went to the Kissing Place to wait for Little Hooters. From the Kissing Point ledge I had a clear view of the Gulf of

Mexico and sat watching the large, orange, beaver moon set over the horizon. Watching alone made me feel sad, and I wished that Little Hooters were next to me sharing the view.

How many more of these sad, lonely experiences will I endure in the future?

Little Hooters arrived about ten minutes later. She had obviously gotten some rest and cleaned up, and she looked much better. I hugged her, and we kissed just as the last sliver of moon disappeared below the horizon.

"I cannot tell Jumping Jack of my decision—that I choose you over him. Not until he is better. But my parents and the elders are pressuring me to make my announcement. Everyone wants me to choose Jumping Jack, not you," she said.

"He won the contest fair and square. He is the better warrior. You must marry the better warrior," I said.

"I told you before, the result of the warrior games is not binding on me. I have made my choice to marry you. But you could have made my decision more acceptable to the people if you had won the challenges."

She squeezed me tightly around my waist.

"Little Hooters, I asked you here tonight because I must tell you something. I can wait no longer to tell you. I will not marry you."

It broke my heart to say that to her and to see the look of pain and disbelief on her face.

"What are you talking about? You love me and I love you! That is all that matters—not what people think!"

"No. I don't love you like that, Little Hooters." I could not look at her eyes as I spoke my lie.

"Why are you doing this? Why are you lying to me?" she grabbed my face and forced me to look into her eyes.

"I love the ocean. I love living as free as the wind. I love traveling the land and ocean more than I love being tied down with you. You would be my anchor. You would only bog me down."

I hated myself for acting so cruel, but I had no other way to terminate our relationship without further debate. I thought of the vision of sorrow to remind me that I was being cruel out of love for Little Hooters. I was lying and rejecting her to protect her, not to hurt her. I feared that if I listened to her any longer, I would be too weak to end our relationship.

"Are you doing this out of pity for Jumping Jack? Even *you* said he would get better." She was crying again.

"No, I'm doing this for myself. I don't want a woman getting in my way and controlling my life. I want to flow with the tides and chase the setting sun without you as a ball and chain—as my anchor."

I tried my best to act cold and uncaring, but it was killing me inside and breaking my heart.

"What happened to you out there in the swamp? I hardly recognize you. You are like a different person." She was truly shocked by my attitude and behavior.

"There is no mystery here, woman. I just don't want to spend my life with a ball and chain. Tell the people that you will marry Jumping Jack. We have nothing more to discuss."

My heart broke as I walked away, leaving the woman I loved kneeling on the ground and sobbing in the dark, moonless night.

That night I lay upon the deck of the *Watermelon* beside Melon Dog, looking up at my old friend Orion, the great hunter of the night sky. Wiping a tear from my cheek, I asked him, "Why did you make me hurt the woman I love, the only person I love more than my own life?"

A voice in my head spoke out. "Will you talk to me yet?"

I looked at the dog and could no longer deny that it was he that was communicating with me. This time the voice in my head was a welcome distraction from my suffering.

"I have learned the magic of my Indian friends, Melon Dog—the magic of talking with animals!"

"It is not magic, master. It is a sixth sense available to people who choose to practice it."

I noticed that the dog was now communicating with me without barking. It was nice to have someone to talk with, but I was still not completely certain that I wasn't simply delusional. The possibility that I was entering the realm of insanity was actually a relief, an explanation and justification of why I could not be with Little Hooters.

"I just ended my relationship with Little Hooters. I need to leave the Watchacallit village. I cannot bear to see her now. My heart is broken, and so is hers," I said to the dog.

"Take a load of crafts to Miami. I will go with you. We will take a load of crafts to trade, but then you must help me find my young master, Luca, his real name is Lucas but he likes Luca. The young boy is my true master, but the boy is in great danger from his cruel father. I love Lucas, and we must help him."

"That is a good excuse for me to get away. You're a clever dog, Melon! With any luck, we can sail in two days' time, my friend!"

A dog is man's best friend!

Chapter 23

THE FEAST OF LONGEVITY

SUNDAY, NOVEMBER 18ᵀᴴ, 1973

Little Hummingbird paid me a visit. She told me that Little Hooters was angry and heartbroken. Little Hooters could not understand why I had rejected her. Little Hummer told me that the responsibility for the care of Jumping Jack was keeping Little Hooters very busy, and that it was a benefit to her.

I had been keeping my distance from the medicine hut because I did not want another confrontation with Little Hooters. Seeing her would only cause both of us more pain and heartache. Now, two days had passed since I had spoken to Little Hooters at the Kissing Point, and I had been in no mood for any company. I had isolated myself on the *Watermelon*.

It was in the early afternoon that Running Deer came to visit me. "Hey, hey, hey! Sun Chaser!" When Running Deer called to me from the beach, I was below deck.

Hey, hey, Running Deer, come aboard."

He walked up the gangway and boarded. "People are worried. No one has seen you for days," he said as he hopped onto the deck.

"I have been in no mood to socialize. Little Hooters and I have parted ways," I said.

"Everyone knows about that. You bring great honor to yourself for stepping aside to the superior Whatchacallit warrior. You are being held in high esteem and great honor by the tribe for bowing out to Jumping Jack. All the elders are talking about your magnanimous character. They are saying that one day Sun Chaser might earn the title of wise man and sit among the council."

"I'm afraid I'm receiving undue credit, Running Deer. I had no choice in the matter, no choice in my destiny. If I could, I would marry Little Hooters today."

"You are a humble man. All the warriors are proud of you, Sun Chaser. The elders have asked me to tell you that you have been invited to the Feast of Longevity. You must go to the grand meeting lodge at 5:00 pm to witness the ceremony," said Running Deer.

"What is that—the Feast of Longevity?" I asked.

"A ceremony where the elders will partake of the forbidden fruits and the Wanton wasp honey that you and Jumping Jack brought back to the village. The fruit and honey combination is the secret to the elders' longevity and ability to live far beyond a normal life span."

"Partake? You mean they are going to eat those fruits! They are poisonous—the most toxic things I've seen! A raccoon died in a matter of minutes after taking one bite, and then a gator ate the coon carcass and also suddenly died!"

I was horrified at the thought of the elders eating the forbidden, poisonous fruit.

"The elders have the secret—the secret to survive and to grow younger from the sweet fruit and honey. You must not worry. It is a great honor that you have been invited to witness the ceremony. The leaders must have plans for you to one day join the covenant of the wise men and women."

"Tell them I will come."

I heard barking in the forest.

"Hey, hey…it's Melon Dog! Come here, boy!"

Running Deer was excited to see Melon Dog. The dog had been out exploring the forest all day but now came running down the beach toward us, barking excitedly.

"Melon Dog says that you have begun to talk with him! That is good, Sun Chaser. You are learning the Indian ways!"

The collie ran up the gangway and leaped high up to Running Deer's waiting arms. Running Deer caught him and hugged the dog to his chest as Melon licked the man's face.

"Did dog tell you he wants to find his master—the little boy named Lucas?" asked Running Deer.

Now I knew he was communicating with the dog. It was confirmed. I had not told Running Deer the young boy's name, Lucas! That proved that the dog must have told him Lucas's name.

"Yes Running Deer, the dog told me he needs to find Lucas. He even devised a plan, an excuse for us to go to Miami on a trading mission so we can search for the boy."

"I told you! He very smart dog!" Running Deer vigorously rubbed the dog's head and then added, "I have more good news, Sun Chaser. This morning, Jumping Jack stood upright. He can't really walk yet, but he took a couple of steps. Chief Thunder Butt has announced that the feast honoring Jumping Jack's victory will be held in two days—on Tuesday at sunset in front of the fire pit."

"That's great. Little Hooters will probably make her big wedding announcement," I said bitterly.

"Yes, I think so," he said.

"Running Deer, why don't you take Melon Dog home with you today? I need a little bit of time to be alone."

"Sure, I love hunting with dog! He good hunting dog."

Running Deer sprinted down the beach toward his village with the dog nipping and barking at his heels.

At 4:30 pm I began walking toward the grand meeting lodge to witness the ceremonial feast of longevity. When I entered the lodge, all twelve of the elders, six men and six women, sat at a long wooden table. The men were on one side and the women on the other. At the end of the table sat Night Owl to the right and Weeping Willow to the left. I was one of only six observers who had been invited to the ceremony. They directed me to sit in the observation bleachers with the other five. I saw Horny Owl, the great-grandson of Weeping Willow, sitting directly in front of me, and decided to warn him about the toxic, forbidden fruit.

"Horny Owl, you must not let your great-grandmother eat that fruit! I saw two animals die from its poison!" I leaned forward and whispered in the creepy young man's ear. The tone of urgency in my voice had no effect on the kid's flat, unemotional demeanor.

"She will not be harmed. The forbidden fruit is deadly to all living creatures that do not have the ability to thwart its toxins and to absorb its magic," said the kid.

"How can these weak, elderly people do that?" I asked.

"To survive the fruit, the first requirement is to be very old. The fruit causes hyper tissue rejuvenation. Cell reproduction and replacement begins to occur at the rate of a gestating fetus. A young or even middle-aged creature will die from this rapid cell growth. The very old and decrepit flourish from the rapid cell replacement and reproduction."

The young man seemed to enjoy sharing his knowledge.

"So is that how Night Owl and your great-grandmom have lived so long? Maybe the rumors of them being over 200 years old are true," I said as I moved forward one row to sit beside the emaciated kid.

"It is true! Two hundred years—but old age is not the only requirement. To survive the fruit and honey one must be very skilled at astral projection."

"What is that, astral projection?"

"It's out-of-body travel, the ability to separate the spirit from the physical body. The conscious mind and spirit would not survive the trauma of this physical rejuvenation, so the elders must temporarily leave their bodies and return only after the parenchyma cell chaos has ceased."

Chief Thunder Butt called for total silence. The elders sat gazing at the ceiling, with palms upturned. One by one they went into a trance and began trembling.

"They have left us. They are out of body," the kid whispered.

Now the chief dipped a spoon into the large bowl of sliced forbidden fruit that had been covered with the magic honey. One by one he fed the elders a spoonful. Each one, upon swallowing the sweet dessert, began shaking violently just as the raccoon had before dying. Before my very eyes I could see muscle tone increasing in their arms, legs, and necks. Even the facial muscles tightened, and their skin gained collagen. All of the twelve elders had been transformed and looked ten to twenty years younger.

"That was amazing!" I gasped.

Now for the first time I understood why the elders had risked the lives of Jumping Jack and me when they sent us out to gather the Forbidden Fruit and Wanton wasp honey. The sweets were the key to their longevity!

After over twenty minutes of shaking and thrashing, one by one the elders went limp and slumped down in their seats, apparently unconscious. Wise men (elders in training) carried them off to recover in the back room of the lodge. The spectacle was over.

"That was the most incredible thing I have ever seen!" I said.

The kid spoke. "Several years from now I will become wise man. Then I will be witch doctor and work with Weeping Willow. After I grow very old I will sit at the Feast of Longevity...just as my grand did today"

The young kid had his whole future planned.

"Thanks for giving me that blow-by-blow description of the ceremony. I would never have understood what was happening. Never known what I just witnessed."

Once outside the lodge, I slapped the kid's shoulder to thank him. "Whatchacallit!"

The gesture was meant as a compliment, but the frail kid looked like he was about to cry. "You warriors are uncouth, crude barbarians. Leave me alone or I'll put a spell on you!" The frail boy walked away, rubbing his shoulder.

"Sorry, kid. I was trying to make friends. You're very smart, and a good kid, too!"

I tried to make amends and soothe his pain, I didn't want to make him an enemy or become a victim of his black magic.

A soft word turneth away wrath

Chapter 24

FAREWELL TO LOVE

MONDAY, NOVEMBER 19ᵀᴴ, 1973

From the northwest, a cold front was pushing across the Florida peninsula. The weather on this autumn morning reflected my mood: dreary, gray, and cold. A light, misty rainfall chilled me to the bone. The weather reminded me of the gray winter mornings I had often experienced in the Northeast. Finding refuge below deck, I had just finished making a pot of hot coffee when someone called me from the beach.

"Sun Chaser, are you home?" I poked my head out to see who it was and was shocked to see Jumping Jack standing alone on the beach.

"What are you doing out and about? Come in here! Get out of the rain!" I was not happy to see him soaking wet and standing in the cold rain. He came aboard, and we went below deck.

"Here, drink some hot coffee," I said.

"Mmm, good! You make good coffee—like woman." Jumping Jack's color and sense of humor were beginning to return, but he still looked frail.

"How did you get away from Night Owl and Little Hooters?" I asked as I threw a towel in his face.

"They not see me. I sneak out when they go into back room...I have to hide. They sure to be mad at Jumping Jack!" he said.

"I was worried about your spine. When did you start walking on your own?"

"Today first time walk. I walk plenty good. The wasp poison is almost gone from me."

He showed me the nasty-looking wound, a red circle surrounding black, necrotic flesh, and in the center a deep depression where the massive stinger had punctured his back. The damage was sure to leave a permanent, ugly scar.

"That looks nasty...painful! You are a madman, Jumping Jack. You're indomitable! You should be in bed resting!"

"What that mean, indom...able?" he seemed to think it was an insult.

"That means you are a man who thinks he is invincible. You think you are an immortal, but you're not!" I said and gave him a refill.

"Tonight I be honored at feast. Little Hooters will make her choice. Her parents have told me that she choose me, but I know that she want choose you. I do not want to marry woman who loves another. I came to tell you that you do not have to let her choose me if you want her. I think she would choose you, not me, if you tell her you want her." He spoke slowly; there was sadness in his voice.

"No! I'm leaving for a while, Jumping Jack—leaving even before your ceremony tonight. Sorry, but I cannot bear to see Little Hooters again. It is dangerous for me to see her."

I could tell that Jumping Jack did not understand why I said it was dangerous, but he did not question my decision to leave, and he seemed to be glad.

"Sun Chaser, you have brought our people out of the shadows. You have taught the people they need not live in fear and that not all Wasichu people are evil. You have shown us how to trade with the outsiders, and our people are happy. You must come back to us soon, Sun Chaser Eddie Ocean. Jumping Jack *orders* you to come back very soon!" To my amazement Jumping Jack hugged me.

"Now Jumping Jack is going soft. Wasp poisons make Jumping Jack soft." I mocked him by mimicking the reaction he had when I hugged him in front of Little Hooters and Night Owl.

A voice called to me from the shore. Hey, hey, hey! Sun Chaser Eddie Ocean, have you seen Jumping Jack?"

I poked my head out of the cuddy cabin and looked toward the beach, where three Whatchacallit warriors were standing in a row. Jumping Jack hid under my bedroll by pulling the covers up over his head, then he peeked out from under the blanket and put his finger to his lips, signaling me to not tell on him.

"Ahhh...well, no! Isn't he in the medicine hut recovering?" I lied for my mischievous friend.

"Jumping Jack not at medicine hut. He ran away! If you see him, bring him back to the medicine hut. He in heap big trouble! Little Hooters and Night Owl plenty angry!"

The trio ran off into the forest to search for Jumping Jack.

"You better go back. Things will only get worse for you," I advised.

"Nothing worse than the wrath of a Whatchacallit woman! I hide in the fishing camp until start of feast. Then the crowd honoring Jumping Jack will protect Jumping Jack...protect me from Little Hooters' scolding!"

Jumping Jack peeked out of the cuddy cabin to see if it was safe to leave. He had a smirk on his face and seemed to be enjoying his game of hide-and-seek. He walked, stiffly and with a limp, down the beach toward his home in the fishing village.

By mid-afternoon, the cold front had pushed through, and the sky became sunny and clear. The air was cool with a light breeze. It was a perfect, beautiful autumn day. Melon Dog returned to the boat at about 3:00 pm, and I tried to communicate with him but he had gone silent, a state of incommunicado that Running Deer had told me happens often with all the animals in the kingdom.

I began making preparations to sail. I wanted to leave with the outgoing tide. The ebb tide would begin just before sunset, just as Jumping Jack's celebration was scheduled to begin.

Suddenly a voice was in my head again. "I dreamed of Lucas last night. As I slept beside Running Deer I saw Lucas in my dream. The boy is in great danger, and we must find him as soon as possible." It was Melon Dog, breaking his silence.

"We will sail with the outgoing tide, in about two hours. Then we have a four-day journey to Miami—that is the best I can do."

"I fear we will not make it in time to help my master!" The dog looked nervous as he paced back and forth on the deck.

The sun was low in the sky, and by the ripple on the water's surface, I recognized the beginning of the outgoing tide. On shore I released a safety line that was tied to the mangroves and prepared to cast off. Suddenly, an urge to delay my departure came over me.

Walking back to a mangrove tree to which my boat had been tied, I pulled off a leaf, broke it in half, and smelled the familiar scent of its oil. Then I lightly ran the tips of my fingers over the rough trunk of a tall coconut palm. I stood on the beach and slowly turned in a complete circle, taking a mental, panoramic picture of the Whatchacallit kingdom, my new home, and the place that I had grown to love so very much. I noticed Melon Dog looking at me with an expression that seemed to ask, "What the heck is wrong with *you?*"

I bent down and picked up a fistful of white beach sand and smelled its blended aroma, the earth mixing with the ocean. I put a handful of the fine, white sand in my pocket and then began to untie the boat. I would miss this place dearly and had no idea if I would ever return.

"Were you going to leave without saying goodbye?'

I was surprised to see Little Hooters walking out of the forest and onto the beach. She looked beautiful, framed by the lush forest as she walked down the path leading to my dock.

"Yes, I'm leaving. I did not want to bring you any more pain. I never meant to hurt you. I will never forget you, and you will always be my friend," I said.

She stood very close, directly in front of me, stiffly and with clenched fists. "I know you love me, Sun Chaser Eddie Ocean! You are not fooling me. I do not know why you are doing this to us—but I know you must have your reasons."

She unclenched her fists; for the first time she seemed to have reached a state of acceptance. She no longer tried to persuade me and change my decision.

There was an awkward silence, and then I spoke. "I will always be your friend. I will think of you when I see the moon above. No matter where I travel, I will know that you can see the moon too. The moon will remind us of our first kiss beneath it. The moon can be something we still share together, no matter where we are."

I leaned forward and kissed her forehead. I could smell the sweetness of the flowers in her hair. A glow, an aurora appeared, framing her beautiful face and radiating warmth. Her beauty and inner light threatened to melt my icy façade. I had intended to act cold and indifferent, but I was being seduced all over again. I knew that I needed to leave pronto! She did not attempt to hug me or stop me as I turned away and untied my boat. I hopped onboard and started motoring away, down the canal.

In the distance to the east, I heard wild drumming coming from the village. Jumping Jack's ceremony had commenced. I looked ahead to the west into the Gulf and saw the sun beginning to set on the horizon. Looking astern for the last time, I saw Little Hooters sitting on the white sandy beach. She had a blank, unemotional expression—she must have been all cried out, but I wasn't. The pure, white sand was the perfect backdrop to frame her beautiful brown skin and jet-black hair. She was illuminated by the soft, orange, light of the sunset, and she seemed to glow like an angel. The space rock that I had given to her rested on her chest, just to right of her heart, and it sparkled in the twilight. For the last time, I looked at the woman I loved and burned her image into my memory. I feared that one day I might forget how beautiful she was.

I aimed the bow of the *Watermelon* directly at the setting sun. It was now a semicircle, halfway below the horizon. Through my teary eyes, the orange sunlight shimmered, and the wetness blurred my vision. Melon Dog stood at the bow, straight as an arrow in a pointer's stance. Like the needle on my compass, he directed my course.

"Go ahead and chase the sun! Go ahead, Sun Chaser Eddie Ocean—follow your destiny! But one thing you must know: I will always love you!" Little Hooters called to me from the beach.

Not daring to respond or even look back, out of fear that my broken heart might convince me to turn the boat around, I continued sailing westward toward the sunset. I wiped away my tears as the last sliver of sunshine disappeared below the horizon. The sky above it exploded with beams of light reaching toward the heavens, a kaleidoscope of colors and hue, red, purple and orange rays fanned out over the horizon.

"Well, Melon Dog, my love is lost—now yours must be found. We will find the boy you love. We will return to Miami to find your master. We will find Luca!"

Mick Dagger told us in a song

You can't always get what you want

The End

Hialeah Florida 1974.

From left to right, E.O. Test with his friend Major upon whom Jumping Jack's character was based.

www.ingramcontent.com/pod-product-compliance
Lightning Source LLC
Chambersburg PA
CBHW031326170626
46807CB00002B/585